LEARNING TO F

Christopher Hope was born in Johannesburg and grew up in Pretoria. He was educated at the Universities of Witwatersrand and Natal. His first book of poems was *Cape Drives* (1974), which received the Cholmondeley Award, and his first novel, *A Separate Development* (1980), won the David Higham Prize for Fiction in 1981. His long poem *Englishmen* was dramatised by the BBC in 1986. His next novel, *Kruger's Alp*, won the Whitbread Prize for Fiction in 1985, and the *Hottentot Room* was published the following year. *Black Swan*, a novella, followed in 1987, and in 1988 he published his first work of non-fiction, *White Boy Running*, which won the CNA Award in 1989. *Learning to Fly* under its original title *Private Parts and Other Tales*, was given the International P.E.N. Silver Pen Award in 1982. Christopher Hope has lived in London since 1975.

Also by Christopher Hope

Fiction

A Separate Development*
Kruger's Alp
The Hottentot Room
Black Swan
My Chocolate Redeemer*

Non-fiction

White Boy Running

Poetry

Cape Drives
In the Country of the Black Pig
Englishmen

For Children

The King, the Cat and the Fiddle
The Dragon Wore Pink

* *Available in Minerva*

CHRISTOPHER HOPE

Learning to Fly

Minerva

A Minerva Paperback

LEARNING TO FLY

First published in Great Britain 1982
as *Private Parts and Other Stories*
by Routledge & Kegan Paul Ltd
This Minerva edition published 1990
by Mandarin Paperbacks
Michelin House, 81 Fulham Road, London SW3 6RB

Minerva is an imprint of the Octopus Publishing Group

Copyright © Christopher Hope 1982

A CIP catalogue record for this book
is available from the British Library
ISBN 0 7493 9043 3

Printed in Great Britain
by Cox & Wyman Ltd, Reading

This book is sold subject to the condition
that it shall not, by way of trade or otherwise,
be lent, resold, hired out, or otherwise circulated
without the publisher's prior consent in any form
of binding or cover other than that in which
it is published and without a similar condition
including this condition being imposed
on the subsequent purchaser.

For Phil Joffe

*A foutra for the world and worldlings base.
I speak of Africa and golden joys.*

Henry IV, Pt 2

Contents

Learning to Fly   1
An Immaculate Conception   11
The Problem with Staff   25
Arthur: Or The Man Who Was Afraid of Nothing   41
Ndbele's People   56
On the Frontier   84
My Stigmata   101
The Kugel   110
Carnation Butterfly   125
Hilton Hits Back   133
The Fall of the British Empire   156
Whatever Happened to Vilakazi?   171

Learning to Fly

Long ago, in the final days of the old regime, there lived a colonel who held an important job in the State Security Police and his name was Rocco du Preez. Colonel du Preez was in charge of the interrogation of political suspects and because of his effect on the prisoners of the old regime he became widely known in the country as 'Window jumpin'' du Preez. After mentioning his name it was customary to add 'thank God', because he was a strong man and in the dying days of the old regime everyone agreed that we needed a strong man. Now Colonel du Preez acquired his rather strange nickname not because he did any window jumping himself but rather because he had been the first to draw attention to this phenomenon which affected so many of the prisoners who were brought before him.

The offices of State Security were situated on the thirteenth floor of a handsome and tall modern block in the centre of town. Their high windows looked down on to a little dead-end street far below. Once this street had been choked with traffic and bustling with thriving shops. Then one day the first jumper landed on the roof of a car parked in the street and after that it was shut to traffic and turned into a pedestrian shopping mall. The street was filled in and covered over with crazy paving and one or two benches set up for weary shoppers. However, the jumpings increased. There were sometimes one or two a week and several nasty accidents on the ground began to frighten off the shoppers.

Whenever a jump had taken place the little street was cordoned off to allow in the emergency services: the police, the undertaker's men, the municipal workers brought in to hose down the area of impact which was often surprisingly large. The jumpings were bad for business and the shopkeepers grew desperate. The authorities were sympathetic and erected covered walk-ways running the length of the street leaving only the central area of crazy pavings and the benches, on which no one had ever been known to sit, exposed to the heavens; the walk-ways protected by their overhead concrete parapets were guaranteed safe against any and all flying objects. But still trade dwindled as one by one the shops closed, and the street slowly died and came to be known by the locals, who gave it a wide berth, as the 'landing field'.

As everyone knows, window jumpings increased apace over the years and being well placed to study them probably led Colonel Rocco du Preez to his celebrated thesis afterwards included in the manual of psychology used by recruits at the Police College and known as du Preez's Law. It states that all men, when brought to the brink, will contrive to find a way out if the least chance is afforded them and the choice of the means is always directly related to the racial characteristics of the individual in question. Some of du Preez's remarks on the subject have come down to us, though these are almost certainly apocryphal, as are so many tales of the final days of the old regime. 'Considering your average white man,' du Preez is supposed to have said, 'my experience is that he prefers hanging – whether by pyjama cord, belt, strips of blanket; providing he finds the handy protuberance, the cell bars, say, or up-ended bedstead, you'll barely have turned your back and he'll be up there swinging from the light cord or some other chosen noose. Your white man in his last throes has a wonderful sense of rhythm – believe me, whatever you may have heard to the contrary – I've seen several Whites about to cough it and all of them have been wonderful dancers. Your Indian, now, he's something else, a slippery customer who prefers smooth surfaces. I've known Asians to slip and crack their skulls in a shower cubicle so narrow you'd have sworn a man couldn't turn in it. This innate slitheriness is probably what makes them good businessmen. Now, your Coloured, per contra, is more clumsy a character altogether. His hidden talent lies in his amazing lack of co-ordination. Even the most sober rogue can appear hopelessly drunk to the untrained eye. On the surface of things it might seem that you can do nothing with him; he has no taste for the knotted strip of blanket or the convenient bootlace; a soapy bathroom floor leaves him unmoved – yet show him a short, steep flight of steps and he instinctively knows what to do. When it comes to Africans I have found that they, perverse as always, choose another way out. They are given to window jumping. This phenomenon has been very widespread in the past few years. Personally, I suspect its roots go back a long way, back to their superstitions – i.e. to their regard for black magic and witchcraft. Everyone knows that in extreme instances your average blackie will believe anything; that his witchdoctors will turn the white man's bullets to water; or, if he jumps out of a window thirteen stories above terra firma he will miraculously find himself able to fly. Nothing will stop him once his mind's made up. I've seen up to six Bantu jump from a high window on one day. Though the first landed on his head and the others saw the result they were not deterred. It's as if despite the evidence of their senses they believed that if only they could practise enough they would one day manage to take off.'

'Window jumpin'' du Preez worked in an office sparsely furnished with an old desk, a chair, a strip of green, government-issue carpet, a very large steel cabinet marked 'Secret' and a bare, fluorescent light in the ceiling. Poor though the furnishings were, the room was made light and cheerful by the large windows behind his desk and nobody remembers being aware of the meanness of the furnishings when Colonel du Preez was present in the room. When he sat down in his leather swivel chair behind his desk, witnesses reported that he seemed to fill up the room, to make it habitable, even genial. His reddish hair and green eyes were somehow enough to colour the room and make it complete. The eyes had a peculiar, steady glint to them. This was his one peculiarity. When thinking hard about something he had the nervous habit of twirling a lock of the reddish hair, a copper colour with gingery lights, in the words of a witness, around a finger. It was his only nervous habit. Since these were often the last words ever spoken by very brave men, we have to wonder at their ability to register details so sharply under terrible conditions; it is these details that provide us with our only glimpse of the man, as no photographs have come down to us.

It was to this office that three plainclothes men one day brought a new prisoner. The charge-sheet was singularly bare: it read simply, 'Mpahlele ... Jake. Possession of explosives'. Obviously they had got very little out of him. The men left closing the door softly, almost reverently, behind them.

The prisoner wore an old black coat, ragged grey flannels and a black beret tilted at an angle which gave him an odd, jaunty, rather continental look, made all the more incongruous by the fact that his hands were manacled behind him. Du Preez reached up with his desk ruler and knocked off the beret revealing a bald head gleaming in the overhead fluorescent light. It would have been shaved and polished, du Preez guessed, by one of the wandering barbers who traditionally gathered on Sundays down by the municipal lake, setting up three-legged stools and basins of water and hanging towels and leather strops for their cutthroat razors from the lower branches of a convenient tree and draping their customers in large red and white check cloths, giving them little hand mirrors so that they could look on while the barbers scraped, snipped, polished and gossiped away the sunny afternoon by the water's edge beneath the tall bluegums. Clearly Mpahlele belonged to the old school of whom there were fewer each year as the fashion for Afro-wigs and strange woollen bangs took increasing hold among younger Blacks. Du Preez couldn't help warming to this just a little. After all, he was one of the old school himself in the new age of trimmers and ameliorists. Mpahlele was tall, as tall as du Preez and, he reckoned, about the same age – though it was always difficult to tell with Africans. A knife scar ran from his right eye down to his collar, the flesh fused in a livid welt as if a tiny mole had burrowed under the black skin pushing up a furrow behind it. His nose had been broken, too, probably as the result of the same township fracas, and had mended badly turning to the left and then sharply to the right as if unable to make up its mind. The man was obviously a brawler. Mpahlele's dark brown eyes were remarkably calm – almost to the point of arrogance, du Preez thought for an instant, before dismissing the absurd notion with a tiny smile. It shocked him to see an answering smile on the prisoner's lips. However he was too old a hand to let this show.

'Where are the explosives?'

'I have no explosives,' Mpahlele answered.

He spoke quietly but du Preez thought he detected a most unjustifiable calm amounting to confidence, or worse, to insolence, and he noted how he talked with special care. It was another insight. On his pad he wrote the letters MK. The prisoner's diction and accent betrayed him: Mission Kaffir. Raised at one of the stations by foolish clergy as though he was one day going to be a white man. Of course, the word 'kaffir' was not a word in official use any longer. Like other names at that time growing less acceptable as descriptions of Africans: 'native', 'coon' and even 'Bantu', the word had given way to softer names in an attempt to respond to the disaffection springing up among black people. But du Preez, as he told himself, was too old a dog to learn new tricks. Besides, he was not interested in learning to be more 'responsive'. He did not belong to the ameliorists. His job was to control disaffection and where necessary to put it down with proper force. And anyway, his notes were strictly for his own reference, private reminders of his first impressions of a prisoner, useful when, and if, a second interview took place. The number of people he saw was growing daily and he could not expect to keep track of them all in his head.

Du Preez left his desk and slowly circled the prisoner. 'Your comrade who placed the bomb in the shopping centre was a bungler. There was great damage. Many people were killed. Women and children among them. But he wasn't quick enough, your friend. The blast caught him too. Before he died he gave us your name. The paraffin tests show you handled explosives recently. I want the location of the cache. I want the make-up of your cell with names and addresses as well as anything else you might want to tell me.'

'If the bomb did its business then the man was no bungler,' Mpahlele said.

'The murder of women and children – no bungle?'

Mpahlele shrugged. 'Casualties of war.'

Du Preez circled him and stopped beside his right ear. 'I don't call the death of children war. I call it barbarism.'

'Our children have been dying for years but we have never called it barbarism. Now we are learning. You and I know what we mean. I'm your prisoner of war. You will do whatever you can to get me to tell you things you want to know. Then you will get rid of me. But I will tell you nothing. So why don't you finish with me now? Save time.' His brown eyes rested briefly and calmly on du Preez's empty chair, and then swept the room as if the man had said all he had to say and was now more interested in getting to know that notorious office.

A muscle in du Preez's cheek rippled and it took him a moment longer than he would have liked to bring his face back to a decent composure. Then he crossed to the big steel cabinet and opened it. Inside was the terrible, tangled paraphernalia of persuasion, the electric generator, the leads and electrodes, the salt water for sharpening contact and the thick leather straps necessary for restraining the shocked and writhing victim. At the sight of this he scored a point; he thought he detected a momentary pause, a faltering in the steady brown eyes taking stock of his office, and he pressed home the advantage. 'It's very seldom that people fail to talk to me after this treatment.' He held up the electrodes. 'The pain is intense.'

In fact, as we know now, the apparatus in the cabinet was not that actually used on prisoners – indeed, one can see the same equipment on permanent exhibition in the National Museum of the Revolution. Du Preez, in fact, kept it for effect. The real thing was administered by a special team in a soundproof room on one of the lower floors. But the mere sight of the equipment, whose reputation was huge among the townships and shanty towns, was often enough to have the effect of loosening stubborn tongues. However, Mpahlele looked at the tangle of wires and straps as if he wanted to include them in his inventory of the room and his expression suggested not fear but rather – and this du Preez found positively alarming – a hint of approval. There was nothing more to be said. He went back to his desk, pressed the buzzer and the plainclothes men came in and took Mpahlele downstairs.

Over the next twenty-four hours 'Window jumpin'' du Preez puzzled over his new prisoner. It was a long time before he put his finger on some of the qualities distinguishing this man from others he'd worked with under similar circumstances. Clearly, Mpahlele was not frightened. But then other men had been brave too – for a while. It was not only bravery, one had to add to it the strange fact that this man quite clearly did not hate him. That was quite alarming: Mpahlele had treated him as if they were truly equals. There was an effrontery about this he found maddening and the more he thought about it, the more he raged inside. He walked over to the windows behind his desk and gazed down to the dead little square with its empty benches and its crazy paving which, with its haphazard joins where the stones were cemented one to the next into nonsensical, snaking patterns, looked from the height of the thirteenth story as if a giant had brought his foot down hard and the earth had shivered into a thousand pieces. He was getting angry. Worse, he was letting his anger cloud his judgment. Worse still, he didn't care.

Mpahlele was in a bad way when they brought him back to du Preez. His face was so bruised that the old knife scar was barely visible, his lower lip was bleeding copiously and he swayed when the policemen let him go and might have fallen had he not grabbed the edge of the desk and hung there swaying. In answer to du Preez's silent question the interrogators shook their heads. 'Nothing. He never said *nothing*.'

Mpahlele had travelled far in the regions of pain and it had changed him greatly. It might have been another man who clung to du Preez's desk with his breath coming in rusty pants; his throat was choked with phlegm or blood he did not have the strength to cough away. He was bent and old and clearly on his last legs. One eye was puffed up in a great swelling shot with green and purple bruises, but the other, he noticed with a renewed spurt of anger, though it had trouble focusing, showed the same old haughty gleam when he spoke to the man.

'Have you any more to tell me about your war?'

Mpahlele gathered himself with a great effort, his one good eye flickering wildly with the strain. He licked the blood off his lips and wiped it from his chin. 'We will win,' he said, 'soon.'

Du Preez dismissed the interrogators with a sharp nod and they left his presence by backing away to the door, full of awe at his control. When the door closed behind them he stood up and regarded the swaying figure with its flickering eye. 'You are like children,' he said bitterly, 'and there is nothing we can do for you.'

'Yes,' said Mpahlele, 'we are your children. We owe you everything.'

Du Preez stared at him. But there was not a trace of irony to be detected. The madman was quite plainly sincere in what he said and du Preez found that insufferable. He moved to the windows and opened them. It was now that, so the stories go, he made his fateful remark. 'Well, if you won't talk, then I suppose you had better learn to fly.'

What happened next is not clear except in broad outline even today, the records of the old regime which were to have been made public have unaccountably been reclassified as secret, but we can make an informed guess. Legend then says that du Preez recounted for his prisoner his 'theory of desperate solutions' and that, exhausted though he was, Mpahlele showed quickening interest in the way out chosen by white men – that is to say, dancing. We know this is true because du Preez told the policemen waiting outside the door when he joined them in order to allow Mpahlele to do what he had to do. After waiting a full minute, du Preez entered his office again closing the door behind him, alone, as had become customary in such cases, his colleagues respecting his need for a few moments of privacy before moving on to the next case. Seconds later these colleagues heard a most terrible cry. When they rushed into the room they found it was empty.

Now we are out on a limb. We have no more facts to go on. All is buried in obscurity or say, rather, it is buried with du Preez who plunged from his window down to the landing field at the most horrible speed, landing on his head. Jake Mpahlele has never spoken of his escape from Colonel 'Window jumpin'' du Preez. All we have are the stories. Some firmly believe to this day that it was done by a special magic and Mpahlele had actually learnt to fly and that the colonel on looking out of his window was so jealous at seeing a black man swooping in the heavens that he had plunged after him on the supposition, regarded as axiomatic in the days of the old regime, that anything a black man could do, a white man could do ten times better. Others, more sceptical, said that the prisoner had hidden himself in the steel cabinet with the torture equipment and emerged to push du Preez to hell and then escaped in the confusion you will get in a hive if you kill the queen bee. All that is known for sure is that du Preez lay on the landing field like wet clothes fallen from a washing line, terribly twisted and leaking everywhere. And that in the early days of the new regime Jake Mpahlele was appointed chief investigating officer in charge of the interrogation of suspects and that his work with political prisoners, especially white prisoners, was soon so widely respected that he won rapid promotion to the rank of colonel and became known throughout the country as Colonel Jake 'Dancing'' Mpahlele, and after his name it was customary to add 'thank God', because he was a strong man and in the early days of the new regime everyone agreed we needed a strong man.

An Immaculate Conception

When I was young the biggest ambition of everyone I knew was to be old before his time. Home was a prison, youth a life-sentence and the one hope was to escape in disguise, before you died of teenage. People waited out their time at school impatiently, grew a beerbelly early, began to lose hair, got their driving licences the day they turned eighteen, took a job, any job, and when you bumped into them six months later they already looked thirty. Now, everyone did what he could to speed up the ageing process but mostly these efforts amounted to little more than gestures: there was the popular ploy of proudly letting it be known that, from about the age of eleven, you always did the driving when your family went away on long trips; or the wheeze favoured by the guys who, when they went to a Saturday night party, would make a point of searching out the parents of the host, wherever they had been confined by their ashamed kids for the duration, and spending the evening with them sipping Scotch out of chunky glasses, talking about share prices and the state of the nation.

But there were some who really forged ahead in the race for early middle-age, like Arnie's brother Joseph who had been a few years ahead of me at school anyway, then took a huge leap forward by leaving and going up to the Seminary while still a schoolboy and training to become a priest. At school I remembered him as a tallish chap with lots of fuzzy hair and a thin smile. When I saw him again at Arnie's place, on one of his infrequent home leaves, the transformation was impressive. Suddenly, here was this tubby, large-lipped balding fellow, his ears, now that you could see them, sticking out of the weathered face of a kindly, retired wrestler. His feet, surprisingly tiny in pointed shoes, like shy mice pushed their noses out of his great black bell of a cassock swinging around his ankles. Let me say here and now that Joe was balding better than anyone I knew; the hair had receded from the centre of his head leaving a shiny circle of scalp ringed by crisp brown fluff, like a perfectly pink lake surrounded by thick sedge. It was a natural tonsure, a sign of divine grace almost, rather than simply involuntary balding. The idea wasn't too fanciful because Joe had always been tremendously holy; indeed, one of the favourite jibes of his young brother Arnie, who most emphatically did not get along with him, was that the odour of sanctity followed Joe around like after-shave.

'When we were both small and my mother asked us what we wanted for Christmas, Joe was likely to ask for a hair shirt. If my brother had a hobby, it was praying. Once he made a try for the world praying record. He spent forty solid hours on his knees in The Belfast shop window before he keeled over. He would have done more if he hadn't been fasting. He was always either fainting or fasting, a real saint, old Joe. And a pain in the arse.'

Arnie was spry, very ginger and incurably young. Though only a few years separated the brothers, beside Joseph, the gap was immense; half a lifetime. Arnie's copper-red hair and green eyes gave him a wild look and this was added to by the freckles that swarmed over his face and neck like a thick rust. Arnie's parents, supposing they'd best be grateful for the blessing of their holy son Joe, rather let Arnie do as he liked. What Arnie liked best were parties. It was at one of Arnie's parties that Donald got religion and Merle got Donald.

Donald was another big man about town. He never finished school, just upped and left one day and got himself a job as a window-dresser with *Hector Mackenzies*, which was the smartest men's shop around and soon he had pots of money and was driving around town in an Alfa wearing a variety of fine tweed hacking jackets while we went on dragging to school on our push-bikes. Merle, who had always had big dreams of early, full adult life, took one look at Donald's dove-grey Italian suit with extra wide lapels and double vents, and went crazy with passion. They'd roar across town in his fast car. Donald who'd been greasily dark and rather spotty at school, improved with age when he got to the dress shop. His lank, black hair which had curled limply on his high forehead was slicked back now and he became very precise in his movements, squaring off his gestures with deliberate symmetry, walking carefully with his toes pointing slightly inwards, whistling soundlessly, winking a lot and forever adjusting his tie, with little coughs and caressing his lapels. My friend Maxie Wolferman claimed that he modelled himself, in his sauve, waxen good looks, on the tailors' dummies in *Hector Mackenzie's* window, but then let it be said that Wolfie bore a grudge, because he'd been after Merle himself until Donald smoothed his way onto the scene with his belted mac and his patent leather shoes, gentling a curl on his left temple, and swept her off her feet. You could feel for Wolfie. Merle was most definitely a loss; a small and dainty girl with hair the colour of scrubbed pine, wonderfully square teeth and the most famous breasts for miles around, large without making her at all top-heavy they pushed their way past anything she covered them with, even the sagging blue tunics into which the convent girls were sewn for the sake of modesty. They preceded her like a legend.

It all started when she invited Donald to her school dance and they stayed out all night. After that, they went at it like it was going out of fashion while the rest of us looked on amazed at their daring. They did it in all the usual places, like the parking lot at the Union Buildings but also, according to Donald who was quite open about it, on a pink, bouncy lilo in Merle's swimming pool, for all the world to see except, of course, they made sure it didn't. They grew even wilder and once, because he dared her, they met in the cocktail bar in the Quirinal Hotel with Merle wearing nothing at all but her mother's fur coat and proved it to him when the bar-tender turned his back to splash Worcester sauce into her Bloody Mary. We all followed the affair with excited fascination. Merle presented a strange double life: the demure convent girl cycling to school by day and the wild, blonde bombshell by night tearing around town beside the immaculate Donald, so smooth and sleek he could have been carved out of butter.

Wolfie contended that the business could have only one conclusion. 'That boy is finished,' he told me, 'she's going to trot him down the aisle – mark my words – down the aisle as sure as shooting. A friend of my sister's saw her down at *Young Bride* trying on wedding dresses the other day. Have you seen the bags under his eyes? The guy's being run ragged. He's so tossed out he couldn't fight his way out of a second-hand French letter.'

'Jealousy will get you nowhere.'

'Come on, Morris, I'm serious.'

'Aren't you laying it on a bit? When all's said and done, she's still a schoolgirl.'

He looked at me pityingly. 'Let me tell you, Morris ... Merle may still be *at* school, but her body left some time ago.'

Because he went on about it, I agreed to come along with him and speak to Donald. Donald did not take Wolfie's warning kindly. His handsome, rather sallow face turned darker. He snorted. He cleared his throat several times, lifting his adam's apple, which was a bit prominent, clear of his collar by rearing his head the way a horse does with an uncomfortable bit, at the same time adjusting his beautifully tied Windsor knot in his Paisley tie with excessive delicacy.

'Aren't you just a bad loser, Wolferman? I'm sorry, but it's not my fault if Merle ditched you for me. Anyway, you shouldn't worry. You've got Denyse Esposito.'

The shot went home. Wolfie coloured. The fact was that though he was after Denyse Esposito, the Christian Scientist, the word was that she wasn't 'gettable' short of actual conversion to her faith. But Donald had also been winded by Wolfie's theory; he was caught between feeling flattered that people obviously considered he really *could* marry Merle if he had a mind to, even if the idea had never entered his mind till we told him, and the terrible shock which the thought gave him. At least it made him nervous enough to seek a second opinion.

'What do you think, Morris?'

'The idea is crazy. I mean you couldn't if you wanted to. You're too young – for a start.'

Donald got sniffy about that. 'Correction. Being young is neither here nor there. Yes, I could if I wanted to. The point is that I don't want to.'

'Wanting or not wanting is one thing,' Wolfie announced with silky casualness, 'but then again, some people have been forced.'

The little black curl on Donald's temple jumped up and after several tries at getting it to lie down he licked his finger and glued it into place. Then with a beautiful, wordly-wise sneer he showed us a little golden tin of *Crêpe de Chine*. 'D'you think I don't take precautions? Worry about yourself, Wolferman. Worry about that crazy chick, Esposito. But don't worry about me. I can take care of myself. Me and Merle get on great – that's all . . . now or ever.' He slipped the tin into his trouser pocket where it made a noticeable, tell-tale bulge and I felt quite overcome by his boldness.

If Wolfie was hoping to rattle Donald sufficiently to drive a wedge between him and Merle, then his plan worked in a way. Only it didn't have the results he must have intended. He sowed suspicion in Donald's mind all right and Donald sorted out his suspicions about Merle's intentions in a most unexpected way. He asked her. Whether she was overcome by the grossness of the question or impressed by his candour, I couldn't say, but the fact is she came right back and admitted that, yes, the notion had been going through her mind.

Of course, we didn't know anything about this at the time

but it was soon clear to his public that Donald had gone into a decline. He and Merle still swooped around town in the red Alfa but Donald wore a strained, rather disgruntled look and some people said that they'd actually seen Merle behind the wheel on occasion. Donald developed the habit of trailing off in the middle of a sentence and polishing his rather long front teeth with his forefinger. Merle was as bouncy as ever, eyes bright, hair soft and shining. The contrast between them was startling and apparent to everyone when they came to Arnie's party. The energy Donald lost seemed to pass on to Merle so that, while he looked more wax-like than ever and fidgeted almost continuously with his collar, ears, hair and teeth, she was in the most blooming good health.

I remember that Wolfie and I arrived early at Arnie's place that night despite stopping along the way for a nip of vodka and lemonade Wolfie brought along in a silver hipflask which had belonged to his Uncle Phil who had died in the Battle of Delville Wood. This was a wise precaution on his part because he knew he'd not be allowed any liquor if he was to cut any sort of figure with the teetotal Denyse Esposito. We found Arnie stacking records next to the Gerrard pick-up, looking very depressed. A flight of porcelain ducks arched uncertainly across the wall behind him.

'Grab a beer while the fun lasts,' he directed us to the zinc wash-tub in a corner where bottles of beer and coke floated among bobbing sides of ice. 'When I've got the music going I think I'll go and lie down in a darkened room. You boys will be happy to know my party has the blessing of Holy Mother Church. My dear brother Joseph is on weekend leave from the Belsen on the hill and instead of doing the decent thing and clearing out tonight, he insists on staying behind – to give me what he calls "a hand" – Speak of the Devil – here comes His Grace.'

Togged out in full clerical regalia, black cassock swishing around his ankles, outsize brass crucifix tucked into his waistband in the way a policeman carries his handcuffs, Joseph walked into the room and stood there under the old paper streamers from the previous Christmas and the tangles of fairy lights, smiling warmly and rubbing his hands which were big, with hairy knuckles. I understood Arnie's depression.

'Did he have to wear his frock?' Wolfie whispered.

'Here I am reporting for duty,' Joe beamed and winked. 'Which position do you want me to play, captain?'

Wolfie wandered over with a wicked look in his eye. 'Wouldn't you have felt a bit more comfortable in civvies?' he demanded.

Joe smiled, slow and forgiving. 'I'm like a soldier,' he said, 'this is my uniform. I'm proud of it.'

'Well, please yourself. It's a free country.' Wolfie winked, 'Speaking for myself, I want Denyse Esposito, over there, the one with the bangles and no make-up. She's religious, too.'

I could have died, the bald way Wolfie tried to ride Joseph. It was incredibly rude of him and even Arnie looked away.

Joe smiled gently. 'Desire is a form of prayer – in the right hands. Pray for her, pray *with* her.'

'Prayer isn't exactly what I had in mind,' Wolfie said.

Joe patted his bald head calmly. 'You won't get anywhere without it.'

Wolfie offered him a beer. Joe refused. We wandered away. Clearly Wolfie was thinking hard. 'He looks funny, I grant you, but he 'aint shy,' he said.

Donald arrived in a white suit and buckskin shoes that made him look ghostly with his pale, strained face. Merle was superb and bounced in, fighting fit, swinging a pink vanity case and wearing a pink knitted stole with tassels, and lots of stiff petticoats sticking out in a feathery wave around her pretty knees like a shuttlecock. She held Donald's arm and you could tell her grip was firm because his whole shoulder dipped, spoiling his careful posture. Arnie explained about Joe, and Merle immediately decided that the best thing would be to involve him in the party by getting all the girls to dance with him. Arnie looked grateful. Donald said nothing, he just went on polishing his front teeth with his finger.

I met them among the arctic floes of the beer tub a little later and Merle was not pleased with her lover.

'Shame,' she said. 'Poor thing. He means well. And his manners are quite wonderful. Donald was awful to him, Morris.'

'You called him father,' Donald accused. 'He's not a father yet; he's only got his learner's licence.'

'Well, what should I call him, then?' Merle flashed at him.

'Call him Joe, like I do.'

'Oh you! You've got no shame. Do you know what he did, Morris? He said if ever Joseph changed his mind and pulled out of the priesthood he should pop along to *Hector Mackenzie's* and he'd tog him out for civvy street again. Imagine it! He was so insulting. Only Joseph is too sweet to notice. It's about time you grew up, Donald!' And she waltzed off in a tizzy to find some girlfriends.

Donald looked at me desperately. 'Do you know, Morris. That guy is wearing sandals under his cassock. Toe-capped sandals.'

'I don't suppose they care about fashion and things like that in the Seminary.'

'*Brown* sandals,' he was in agony. 'With blue socks, worn under black. It made me feel ill. Literally sick. I think it's precisely because people don't care about things like that that they end up in the Seminary.'

Arnie came over and caught the bit about the sandals. 'I know, I know. What can I say? Look at him.' We looked at old Joe wretchedly shuffling the records about and mixing up the covers. The flight of ducks soared over his bald patch. 'Isn't he about as wet as the back wall of a urinal?'

I danced a while with Monica Dickson, a hard, lithe blonde but my heart wasn't in it. I watched her springing about like a hard rubber ball and knew it was unlikely I'd ever catch her, or that I could hold her if I did. Wolfie, with typical optimism, claimed to be doing well with Denyse Esposito. Looking a bit embarrassed he said that maybe the priest-guy had got hold of something.

'God works in the strangest ways, Morris. I think religion

is the key to the thing between Denyse and me. We're getting close to trade-off. A couple more glasses of Coke and she'll be all over me, you watch. We're good for each other, see? She wants to convert me and I want to take her clothes off. She wants to talk to me about Mary Baker Eddy and I want to touch her breasts. She says that Christian Science has a true respect for the body. She says God is love. I say – then why don't we enter into a sort of hymn of praise to the body?'

Donald wandered over looking morose and helped himself to another beer. He was really sinking the stuff that night.

Try as she would, Merle drew blanks when she tried to persuade her friends to take a turn around the floor with Joe. In the end, she was the only woman prepared to associate with him. While Donald sat doing his hair-twirling and smoothing his eyebrows and pretending not to notice, Merle helped Joe around the dark floor like a guide dog. Every time I looked Joe was dancing with Merle. He was no good but he hung on gamely while she led him around the room, showing his beaming, apologetic face on one side of her neck then the other and swallowing hard all the time making his adam's apple jump like a live thing above his white collar. Eventually she led him over, sweating happily, to the drinks tub.

'I hope you don't think I am monopolising your young lady,' Joe said to Donald. 'I warned her I was no dancer, but she simply insisted.'

Donald patted him on the head. 'Feel free. You'll be in harness soon. Arnie says you're to be ordained soon. A life of sacrifice. Responsibilities.'

Merle blushed. 'Don't pay attention to him, Joseph.'

Joe gave his mild smile, not at all put out. 'Becoming a priest, as I've told Arnold many times, doesn't mean dying or going to jail. Life begins with ordination, as we say in the seminary. It's my free choice. And choosing is the way we grow up.'

'It's hard to believe that your brother isn't much older

than Donald,' Merle told Arnie. 'He looks so young,' she added confusingly.

'Donald also looks older than he is,' Joe allowed generously.

'Looks are deceptive,' Merle returned grimly, and she tugged at the sleeve of Joe's cassock. 'Like to try again?'

Joe peered at Donald enquiringly. His large forehead was rumpled with kindly, concerned creases. 'Sure you don't mind?'

Donald sucked at his beer and kept his eyes down. 'Feel free.'

It was about half an hour later that I had to break up this strange partnership. I did so at Arnie's insistence. He grabbed me as I passed the record player. 'I'm sick of doing his job. Besides, it's not right for a man pledged to God to be swinging around a darkened room to the music of Ray Conniff, clutched to the most famous pair of charlies this side of Cairo.'

'It's not really his doing, Arnie. Merle virtually kidnapped him. To be fair.'

'To hell with being fair, Morris. Cut in.'

So I sent Joe back to the ducks and the records and took Merle around the floor. She told me I danced wonderfully. Then she asked if I thought Donald was basically immature. Quite seduced by all this flattery, I said I did. It was the right thing to say because she came even closer and poured out her troubles in my ear. She wanted to marry Donald because that seemed the only sensible thing to do. Joseph agreed that this was for the best. He had said so when she told him about their love-affair and how far they'd gone.

'You mean to say you told him about *that*? About the lilo and the fur coat.'

'Don't look so shocked, Morris. Joseph wasn't shocked. He's almost a priest and they're trained. They know more about sex than we do. They have to – they're going to sit in the confessional for the rest of their lives listening to it. Joseph believes I should get married – that we both should.

I told him it would take a miracle. He said he would pray for one.'

At this point Wolfie wandered over with the news of the evening. Donald was missing. He had strolled outside with an armful of beers and never came back. Someone had seen him outside near the summerhouse, much the worse for wear.

Merle took it on the chin, I'll say that for her. Went away and came back with her fringed shawl and a determined look. 'I'll sort him out,' she promised us and we believed her.

'Saw you trying your luck with old Monica. Hard cheese. Slipped away, did she. I swear that girl rubs herself with Vaseline on party nights.' Wolfie grinned sympathetically.

'What's the state of play with Denyse?'

'Getting there.'

'You hope.'

'Scoff away, Morris, you'll see. I'm close to a breakthrough. It's faith that does it. It really does move mountains. I think we'll continue our discussion under the stars. I've been looking down her dress while she explained about God being love and all that. You know what her breasts remind me of? A couple of fat-faced sheep with soft dark noses.' He licked his lips and yawned. 'Ah well, back to work.'

Joseph left a little while later. I think he got tired of playing Frank Chacksfield and Percy Faith records to a group of dancers who had given up all pretence of moving and froze together in corners, or collapsed on sofas or simply stood in the middle of the floor straining together like wrestlers. He marched over and informed Arnie he was going to bed. Arnie made no attempt to conceal his relief and dragged Joe over to me to break the good news.

'Pleasant dreams, old Joe,' he beamed. 'Sleep in tomorrow morning, brother mine. Breakfast in bed, maybe?'

Joe tutted reproachfully. 'Tomorrow is Sunday, Arnold. I will be at six o'clock mass as per usual.' He gave Wolfie an ironical salute. 'I'll say a prayer for you.'

I think Arnie was startled by the grateful look Wolfie

threw Joe as he shuffled out of the room. A few minutes later, Wolfie and Denyse left for the garden.

With his brother out of the way Arnie cheered up and made a desperate effort to make up for lost time. He put on Mantovani, turned the lights down to the sort of glow you get off a wristwatch and made a determined play for the rubbery, elusive Monica and having obviously decided there was no time left for tactics he led her on to the floor and tried the big squeeze. It was hopeless. She broke his grip every time with a simple shrug of her shoulder and he would slide down to about her waist and hang there like a bad ice-skater whose legs have gone their own way. It was too depressing to watch so I got a beer and went outside.

A good three-quarter moon behind thin, fast-moving cloud, threw a steely light on the hushed, warm garden. The music from the party drifted across the lawn and into the thick patches of loquat trees. The corrugated iron roof of the summer-house, tucked away in a far corner beyond the trees, was a mass of crenellated shadows and shining canals down which the moonlight ran and fell into the darkness of the thick, leafy walls. It was the sound of low voices in the summer house that made me step quietly around the back where a tangled wall of ivy screened me. I wasn't ready for what I gradually made out in the dim interior of that little rustic shelter. I am even now, three months later, still not ready for it.

Donald was stretched out on a bench, smiling at the moon and fast asleep. Drunk to the world, let's say. Standing beside him with the moonlight lying like a blessing on his bald crown and making a glimmering ring around his dog-collar, was Arnie's brother Joseph and he was bent over Merle who knelt before him with her forehead inches away from his waistband. Merle and Joseph were muttering at each other in a very strange way and it was some time before I realised what was going on: this was a private religious service. They were praying together. His hand was on her shoulder. She looked up at him. He bent closer. Poor old smashed Donald snored softly beside them and in his pocket

I saw quite clearly the square outline of his precious tin of *Crêpe de Chine*, his 'precautions'. Merle's face was soft and white, like the moon in a mirror. I thought I saw a tear roll down her cheek. Certainly, I saw Joe bend still lower.

I crept away. I stole through the garden. Mingling happily with the soft music from the party there came a contented bleating from a patch of loquat trees and it occurred to me that the night was full of miracles; Wolfie had managed to sell enough of his Jewish soul to Christian Science for Denyse to allow him to play shepherd to her lovely baa-lambs. Even after I'd got home, it was hours before I could stop my hands shaking and think clearly. I was bowled over by the force of what I'd seen: the huge, overpowering determination that is the steel and spring of faith and by the terrible, unarguable brilliance of Merle's conception: desire was a kind of prayer, Joe had told Wolfie, heat chasing hope; but when prayer was answered, as Merle's had been, this order was mysteriously reversed and you were given the deed for the wish, flesh for the word.

I sat next to Wolfie at the wedding and he was a real pain. He wore a browny-green Lurex suit and sat nervously picking the petals off his button-hole all through the nuptial mass. Far from being satisfied that his prophecy had turned out to be true, he was resentful and upset and kept complaining about the length of the service. Donald knelt neatly at the altar. The soles of his new shoes had been carefully blacked, his hair was trimmed and overall he was so scrubbed, clipped and groomed that he was difficult to recognise and he had a distant, faintly tragic look waiting crouched on the altar steps, lonely and vulnerable. Merle arrived in a confident froth of lace accompanied by four suntanned, stalwart bridesmaids in deep apricot. Donald turned slowly to meet his bride and the poor chap took hold fiercely of his earlobe but Merle, gliding into position at his side, slipped her arm through his and put a stop to that.

'I don't understand it,' Wolfie whispered. 'Do you understand it? Donald told me he wants to get married. He's gone mad, Morris. He says he's had a religious experience. This is Donald talking! You know, the guy in the zoot suits, with the red Alfa, with the contraceptives, with sex on the brain . . .! Why are we sitting here? What is going on?'

'I don't know, Wolfie. Unless it's a miracle.'

He stared at me. 'Since when were you a religious fanatic, Morris?'

The reception was made just about bearable by lots of booze. The happy couple didn't stay long before Merle slipped away to change and came back wearing an acid-green 'goingaway' costume that seemed to hurt Donald's eyes because he put his hand in front of his face when he saw her and massaged his sinuses for a long time. I must confess I had eyes for Merle only, even when they climbed into the nuptial Alfa, festooned with tin cans and shaving-soap writing on the windows and which, by common agreement among the bachelors, we did not rock too savagely to speed them on their way because old Donald looked as if he was about to burst into tears: but, as I say, I couldn't keep my eyes off Merle, such a commanding figure in her brilliant green outfit, so poised, balanced, sure of herself, that no one in the crowd, not a soul would have dreamt that she was at that time already three months pregnant – so well did she hold herself.

The Problem with Staff

Mrs Whitney had a soft, oval body, full, yet light as a balloon. Her plump cheeks were flushed from the hotel kitchen in which she worked unceasingly. Her protuberant eyes suggested an overactive thyroid.

Mr Whitney suffered from a cleft palate. He was seldom seen. Though occasionally, the gentle hrumph, hrumph, of his conversation issued from some distant part of the hotel. He had ambitions which outstripped his capital. Generations of guests heard from Mr Whitney of his plans to rebuild the hotel extensively. It would reach thirteen storeys and include a swimming pool, hairdressing salon, restaurant and underground parking garage; the Hotel Board would award it five stars. Drinkers in the hotel's cramped little pub overheard Mr Whitney and Mr Stubb, the chemist, endlessly negotiating the inclusion of a select pharmacy. '... only sunglasses, suntan oil, the Pill – that sort of thing.'

A feature of the hotel was its waiters: Little David, a mulatto; Big David, a huge, apoplectic Indian, and Patrick, an African. As the hotel was small and rarely accommodated more than four guests at a time, the staff, and particularly the waiters, lived lives very close to those of the guests. In the time it took to breakfast, you could learn a lot. Little David's wife had just had a son, Big David drank a good deal, probably out of boredom, and had a bad heart. His wife had left him. Patrick was a bachelor, and this obviously enhanced his status in the eyes of his colleagues since they discussed his pursuits and conquests in loud voices and with much laughter in the dining room between servings.

So far as anyone knew, the waiters had been with the hotel for years. The respectful attitude of the rest of the staff (an elderly Malay woman, named Anne, and three part-time maids) towards them, testified to their authority. Notwithstanding, Mrs Whitney unceasingly complained that they drank, they were dirty, unpunctual, irresponsible and they smelled. Breathlessly, she reviewed the problem of staff for anyone who would listen to her and conclude, inevitably, that they would be the end of her.

They are funny people, said Little David's wife, whose name was Maria, as they were sitting together at home one evening.

That is because they are different, he explained.

Little David's house had one bedroom, a living room and a tiny hallway which they used as a kitchen. The lavatory, a pit latrine, was in the back garden. He had thought once of letting the bedroom to one of the many old men who stumbled about the hotel off-sales and earned their money for wine by doing the odd bit of gardening, dishwashing, poaching and petty thievery and whose very existence in the area was thus a criminal offence, while his presence there was merely illegal. One of them, not too dirty or drunken, would have made a safe tenant. He's had several offers, and no good reason to turn any of them down. Maria had been pregnant and they had needed the money. Perhaps working in a hotel with ten rooms, four bathrooms and two lounges, had gone to Little David's head. Maria thought so. It was illegal to sublet council property. But Little David did not think much of this argument. He and his family were officially classified as Coloureds, and the house stood in that area of Steun Bay reserved exclusively for the use of Indian fishermen who worked for the canning factory. Simply living there was against the law. Little David knew that they would be evicted one day. However, Indian labour was hard to come by, and the canning factory had found it necessary

26

to employ Coloured fishermen, and to house them in the Indian township. Until he'd got the job at the Whitney's hotel, Little David had been a fisherman. He was ambitious. Also, he was reassured by the complexities of the legal situation. When the baby came, he was glad he had kept the room. The Whitneys had given him a rise. Big David had presented him with half a bottle of brandy. One of the guests, a tall German tourist, who heard about it, shook his hand. Patrick had laughed aloud, clapped him on the back, and asked him if he had got his seed back.

At the hotel, Big David was on duty in the dining room. Although the season was well advanced, there were few guests. Mr Whitney had dined alone. It was eight o'clock and David moved from table to table, replacing serviettes, straightening a spoon, and seeing to it that the clusters of plastic flowers stood firmly in their vases on the centre of each table-cloth, and that the water had not evaporated. His movements were sure and deliberate, but his attitude was abstracted. In the warm evening he perspired freely and he was conscious of the sweat collecting in his eyebrows. Midges darted around the tables, and Big David would occasionally pause to flick a dirty serviette into areas of light where they appeared to congregate too thickly. These sudden movements would cause the sweat to run into his eyes. Big David pushed his fist into his eye and rubbed clumsily until the smarting stopped. He felt tired and his feet hurt. Recently, they had become swollen. The doctor had warned him to expect this. The swelling grew worse at night and so Big David, who seldom took much thought for his comfort, bought himself a pair of expensive black leather slippers and wore them around the hotel from six o'clock onward each evening.

His wife, Jayalakshmi, would have laughed at the slippers. Laughed in the way she did at all his fears and aspirations.

The new slippers, she would have said, in much the same tone she had used when he told her of the Whitneys' plans for the new hotel . . . 'of English leather, no doubt?' A tall woman, in an electric blue sari laughing.

When Jayalakshmi left him and went to live with the silk merchant, Naidoo, the Whitneys said nothing, but Big David knew that they were relieved. His wife held positive social and political convictions and liked to express them, often in strong, even strident terms. Her unexpected outbursts alarmed the guests and infuriated the locals in the public bar. Although Big David nearly always agreed with his wife's views in these inflammatory matters, he nevertheless sympathised with the Whitneys, who had their position to maintain. And the more brandy he drank, the more sympathetic he became.

When it was clear that Jayalakshmi would not be returning to him, Mr Whitney drew Big David aside and explained to him his duties in the new hotel.

'You will take charge of the wine stewards in the expanded establishment,' he confided in a solemn susurrus. 'There will be fifteen wine stewards and they will wear bottle-green tunics bearing the hotel's crest emblazoned above the breast pocket, with gold chevrons on the sleeve, striped trousers, bow ties and red fezes. They will all be Indians. Naturally you will be paid more.'

A few days later, the hotel's chambermaid, Anne, met Jayalakshmi in the Capital and in the excitement of their meeting, and perhaps in a belated attempt to effect a reconciliation, told her of Big David's future prospects.

'The chief wine steward?' Jayalakshmi laughed aloud and several people had stared at them. Anne was embarrassed and had wanted to leave, but Jayalakshmi insisted on driving her to the station. Anne submitted, although the size and opulence of the big, black car scandalised her.

On her return, Anne whispered to Big David the details of her meeting with all the ferocity she could muster. The next day he collapsed at the head of the second flight of stairs while on his way to answer a call from an upstairs room.

Big David sighed. After switching off the dining room light he paused by the door just long enough to view the room by moonlight. It usually soothed him, this sight of crisp white table-cloths each precisely surmounted by a vase of flowers, rigorously squared and stapled into position by shining knives and forks. But the scene was without its usual calming effect of glinting metal so neatly related to gleaming white cloth. The dining room had a savage aspect tonight, showing its tables as if it were baring its teeth and they were not neat white teeth held back by impeccably positioned braces, but yellowed stumps, rotting in dark places where the moonlight did not reach, haphazardly stopped with stainless steel.

When Patrick arrived at Beauty's room in the backyard of Mr Stubb's chemist shop, he found about half a dozen men and women already assembled, waiting for the party to begin. Four gallon-jars of white wine stood on a rickety table beside the door. On the floor beside it were two old paraffin tins filled with homebrewed beer. All the women were sitting on the bed. The men leaned against the wall, smoking. There was no sign of Beauty. Patrick took an enamel mug from the table and scooped a measure of beer out of one of the big tins. The place was growing crowded. Two blackened paraffin lamps swung from the ceiling sending shadows climbing up the rough, whitewashed walls. The smell of tobacco, beer and paraffin mingled with the smell of the skin-bleaching cream the women wore on their faces, and filled the room. He moved over to the gramophone which was on the floor beneath the window. Idly he riffled through the tall pile of records beside it. He decided that Beauty must have gone for more beer.

'Atta boy!' someone called encouragingly.

A woman began to tap her feet. Patrick wound the gramophone and dropped a record on the turntable.

'That's *Mister* Monk,' the same voice approved as the first few piano bars slid into the room.

A woman left the bed and began dancing to the music, alone, twitching her bottom, a buttock at a time, to the rhythm. Patrick caught her eye. She waved invitingly.

Patrick glanced about the room. Still no Beauty. Grinning, he rose to his feet and joined the woman.

An hour later, Patrick surveyed the scene again and told himself that the joint was jumping. Nearly two dozen people had crowded themselves into the small room. The bed had been pushed into a corner to make more space. A couple, hopelessly entwined, lay on it. The dancers were sweating freely and every so often the paraffin lamp lighting on a face made it glimmer briefly. Patrick released his partner, who continued to dance alone, and went in search of more beer. The level in the remaining paraffin tin was low, and Beauty had still not appeared. He opened the top half of the door and leaned into the evening breeze. In the darkness somebody was urinating noisily against a wall. A dog barked in the next door yard.

The sound of cheering disturbed him and he turned back into the room to see Beauty standing near the window through which she had apparently just entered. She carried a fresh supply of beer. Patrick grinned. The evening was wonderful. Beauty was wonderful. Smiling happily, he pushed his way towards her.

'Beauty, baby,' he said delightedly.

Beauty stared solemnly up at him.

'Beauty,' he tried again, taking her tin of beer from her and raising it in an expository gesture. 'Mr Booze,' he offered hopefully.

'I have some news for you,' said Beauty grimly.

Mr Whitney was sitting in the hotel's office, beside the desk. He would have sat behind the desk, had he not felt that to do so would have offended his wife, who, since she did the books and paid the accounts, regarded it as her property. In any event, she was going to be badly disturbed by his news. No sense in adding to the confusion, he told himself. Mr Whitney's nose was sleek and sensitive. He rubbed it gently. Then he stood up. He knew what he had to do.

He found his wife in the kitchen, ladle in hand, supervising simmering pots. She eyed her husband cautiously. Mr Whitney came straight to the point.

'I have told Big David that he is to move into the hotel.'

His snuffing voice accorded agreeably with the hissing of the pots.

'For good?' Mrs Whitney asked quietly.

'At least until these attacks of his have stopped. He's had two now, and as you know, the second almost killed him. He can't go on living alone in a miserable room in the native location. He hasn't seen his wife since she ran away with that draper.'

'Why don't you let him go?'

'Be reasonable, Myra!' Mr Whitney decided to be irritable. 'I can't do that. He's a damn good wine steward. How would I replace him? Answer me that. You should know as well as anyone the problems we have finding decent staff for the hotel. Better, in fact. *You're* the one who's always complaining about it. Besides,' his pace slowed, and he articulated more clearly, 'we have a responsibility to our staff. I mean, surely you admit that, hey?'

Mrs Whitney turned her shoulder on this last question, and, taking the lid off one of the pots, peered into it intently. Then abruptly she dropped the lid and faced him, her face pinkened by the steam.

'Sick! You say he's sick. I know his sickness.'

'All right, so he drinks,' Mr Whitney was forcing himself to speak clearly, 'loves his brandy. That's true. The doctor's warned him. Everybody's warned him in his condition it's tantamount to committing suicide.' Gingerly, he touched his wife's shoulder. 'And that's why I want him here at the hotel. I'll keep an eye on him. I'll put a stop to it.'

Mrs Whitney's eyes bulged a little more than they usually did, but she said nothing.

Encouraged in her silence, he stopped for breath. He had put his foot down and he had won. When he began speaking again he fell into his usual manner, half sibilant, half gurgle, the echo of water in an underground cavern, the sound of a scrubbing brush on bare floorboards.

'He can take one of the rooms in the backyard. That way,

he won't actually be in the hotel, but I'll still be able to keep a pretty close watch on him.'

'Let him go,' said Mrs Whitney grimly.

'Then he will die,' Mr Whitney retorted with great force, 'it's not Christian.'

'Let him go.'

'No!'

The pots on the stove reverberated. Mrs Whitney returned her attention to them. Her husband addressed her back: 'There are our plans for the new hotel to consider, Myra.'

Big David found his room behind the hotel very comfortable when Mr Whitney installed him in it the following day. The doctor had prescribed a month's rest after the last attack, and Big David, grateful to Mr Whitney for a place in which to spend the time, was even prepared to tolerate, for as long as he could bear it, Mr Whitney's coming between him and his brandy bottle.

Patrick and Little David did not welcome the extra shifts which in Big David's absence devolved on them, but they did not complain. Mr Whitney was pleased with the results of his plan. Mrs Whitney had not spoken to him, or anybody else, since their interview.

Big David had been resting for five days when, quite suddenly, Jayalakshmi returned. To her husband, she seemed not to have altered in the slightest. Her electric-blue sari billowed generously at her ankles as she strode into his room. His heart gave the tiniest flip when he saw who his visitor was. Instinctively his hand went to his chest. Jayalakshmi's face clouded.

'The invalid!' she cried.

It transpired that Jayalakshmi had left Naidoo. It was an affair she regretted deeply, but, she wished him to know, it was behind her now, dead and forgotten, never to be resurrected. She knew that she could rely on him to respect her wishes. His capacity for respecting the wishes of others was his most endearing quality. To think she had been unaware of his serious illness. But he should understand that she had been out of the country at the time of his first attack. Naidoo went overseas regularly on buying missions. He was still there. She had left him in Bombay. On arriving back she had had news of his condition and come to him immediately. He needed her to look after him. She, Jayalakshmi herself, would nurse him.

Big David lay staring up at her solemn face. She made a concession to his bewilderment. He was wondering about Naidoo, she insisted. He was to do no such thing. It was past foolishness. If he liked he could beat her for it, when he was well again. She paused and looked about Big David's quarters in obvious distaste.

'This is a *mean* little room they have put you in. They have a whole big hotel but they stuff you away here. You, the invalid.'

She seemed not to recall their previous accommodation in the native location some ten miles from the hotel and Big David made no attempt to remind her, but smiled gently.

'They are different from us,' he waved a deprecatory hand.

Jayalakshmi's lip curled and she turned and walked furiously out of the room.

Mr Whitney withstood Jayalakshmi's unexpected return as bravely as he could, but his replies to her questions and accusations were hesitant as if the words would not come out of his mouth and hid behind his damaged palate. He agreed that the little room in the backyard would be too small for both her husband and herself. But at the time he had suggested to Big David that he stay there, he had not anticipated her sudden return. Now he would have to look for something roomier, for the two of them. Always providing, of course, that she intended staying on? But his sarcasm was lost on Jayalakshmi who had begun to shout. Trying desperately to mollify her, he explained that, in the changed circumstances, he would make other plans for accommodating her husband and herself. However he could not agree with her suggestion that the room in the backyard had been too cramped in the first place. It was better than the old room in the location. He reminded her that Big David was ill. Here, help was close at hand. He denied her charge of discrimination, and he informed her that he had effected the move as a kindness, yes, a Christian kindness. He did not hate Indians. He implored her not to shout.

In her office, Mrs Whitney covered her ears as Jayalakshmi's voice cut through the hotel. It was clearly audible in the dining room where Patrick and Little David were laying places for dinner, and they stopped to listen. Little David's admiration for Jayalakshmi swelled inside him.

'Are my husband and I to eat, sleep and excrete in that little pondok,' Jayalakshmi hissed, 'like cattle?'

Grim-faced, Mr Whitney insisted, for the third time, that he realised circumstances had changed and that the room would be too small for both of them. He stressed, however, that until Jayalakshmi's sudden and wholly unexpected return, the arrangements which he had made for her husband's eating and sleeping had satisfied both his doctor and Big David himself. As for the *other* matter which she had seen fit to raise, well, he would point out that separately housed toilet facilities adjoined the room in question. He had no idea where Big David would stay now. He had not thought about it.

'There are plenty of empty rooms on the third floor.'

'But those are guest rooms,' Mr Whitney was shocked.

'And they are always empty,' Jayalakshmi replied placidly.

'For God's sake, woman, I can't let you people stay in the hotel!'

'Why not?'

'It's illegal!'

'It's illegal to have my husband staying in your backyard. I know the law. You have to have a permit from the peri-urban authority if your servants sleep in. I also know, who should know better than I who slept ten years in a filthy, stinking shack in the native location because there was no legal accommodation for my husband within nine miles of his work, I also know that they don't issue living-in permits around here.'

The ground was loosening beneath Mr Whitney's feet. 'I appreciate your concern, and I sympathise, of course. But what can I do about that? You say you know the law. Well then you will know that Indians must stay in the Indian area. Please see my predicament.'

'The predicament is ours,' Jayalakshmi said coldly.

He stared at her impassive face. From the centre of her forehead, her crimson caste-mark glowered angrily at him, he wondered how she kept it in place. He sighed.

An hour later, with the help of his colleagues, Big David was settled comfortably in the largest of the guest rooms on the third floor. Below, kennelled in her office, Mrs Whitney listened to the heavy breathing of the waiters as they struggled up the stairs carrying Big David's bed, scrabbling their way along the landing, urged on by Jayalakshmi's sharp, strident directions towards the patient's triumphant installation. The clang of a chamber pot, a muffled laugh, a series of soft bumps and scrapes as furniture was rearranged and finally, the deep creak of bed-springs. These sounds of Big David's entry into the hotel reached her clearly and scratched themselves on her heart. She trembled with anger.

In the bar, Mr Whitney was having a quiet drink with Mr Stubb.

'Perhaps,' said Mr Stubb, 'the new pharmacy might include a massage parlour. A good hotel needs a massage parlour. And, come to think of it, the masseuse might double up as a counter assistant. No staff problem that way.' So excitedly did he lean forward at the thought of this that the tip of his nose touched Mr Whitney's. 'And such fun, too. Just think of it, our own little masseuse!'

'And no staff problems,' Mr Whitney agreed, 'important that – staff can break you in this game.'

He said nothing to Stubb about Big David's move upstairs. But he was beginning to feel less concerned about it.

He slept well. Mrs Whitney was up and gone before he awoke. She went to market in the Capital on Saturdays. She'd don her one good hat, a faded wreath, and often returned in a better temper.

Patrick waited on him at breakfast. He wasn't his usual smooth, efficient self. Beauty's news had unsettled him. But Mr Whitney did not notice. A fresh problem faced him. Little David had been called home urgently.

He had left shortly before serving breakfast, without an explanation.

He knocked at the door of Big David's room. There was no response. He paused briefly, and then opened the door. Big David was lying propped up in bed with his eyes closed and his hands folded over his fat stomach. Jayalakshmi sat beside him and did not turn when the door opened. To his surprise, he saw Little David in an armchair beside the window. No one acknowledged his presence.

'Well, well, David, I thought that you had been called home?' he remarked in what he hoped was a voice of cheerful enquiry.

Little David opened his mouth but did not seem capable of speech.

'Early this morning the Coloured Affairs Commissioner served an eviction order on him and his family. He must be out of the Indian township within twenty-four hours.' Jayalakshmi's manner was brisk.

Mr Whitney had not left the doorway. 'But where is he to go?'

For a long moment it seemed as if his question would go unanswered.

'In the meantime he will stay here.'

He thought his voice was going to desert him. He struggled with it behind his palate.

'Here,' he managed at last, 'with his family?'

'With his family,' Jayalakshmi answered decisively.

'It's either here or in the Coloured township, nearly twenty miles away,' Big David said softly from his bed, without opening his eyes. 'He's a good waiter. We can't afford to lose him.'

'But not here,' Mr Whitney protested, 'not in the hotel.'

'In the backyard room. The one Big David had,' Little

David implored. '*Please*, Mr Whitney. There is just my wife, the baby and myself. There'll be no trouble.'

'Surely you don't object to that, Mr Whitney?' Jayalakshmi asked, turning to face him for the first time since he had entered the room. 'As my husband and I are no longer occupying the room why shouldn't Little David have it?'

Mr Whitney struggled to control his welling emotions, none of which, he discovered with surprise, resembled any thing approaching anger.

'But it's . . .'

'Illegal!' Jayalakshmi stamped her foot.

It was hopeless. He found that he could not identify his feelings, control his thoughts or even summon up his convictions. Yet, strangely, this somehow seemed not to matter. Jayalakshmi's icy logic cooled his flushed consciousness. The woman was right. The legality of the move was so far removed from the reality of the situation as to make any discussion of it not merely academic, for matters had gone far beyond that, but absurd.

'Of course, you will have to make your own cooking arrangements,' he said.

It was the strong smell of cooking that drew Mrs Whitney to the room in the backyard. A glance through the window was enough. She wheeled and walked furiously back into the hotel, her eyes huge and shining strangely. She found her husband in the damp little lounge, poring over the blueprints of the new hotel.

'I must talk to you,' she said, walking past him and into her office under the stairs.

Mr Whitney took a deep breath, folded up the plans, and followed her. He would show her what dignity was. She slammed the door closed and turned to face him.

'There are Coloured people in the backyard,' she said.

'Why, yes, there are. I had been going to tell you. Since Little David and his family have been summarily evicted from their home, I reflected on the duty of the hotelier towards his staff, and towards his hotel, and I decided to give them permission . . .'

His wife ignored him. 'There are Indians in the hotel itself, in the bedroom above ours.'

Mr Whitney nodded.

'Are you out of your mind?' she shouted suddenly. 'There are now more of them than us on these premises.'

'I fail, absolutely, to see the cause of your alarm.'

His wife was obviously becoming hysterical and he found the sight distasteful. 'After all, they do work here,' he retorted coldly.

'But would you tell me then why they are living here? This is a decent hotel, not a bladdy native location!'

'Myra!' Mr Whitney was shocked.

'What are we going to tell the guests? You must know that it won't be long before they start noticing that we have Indians and Coloureds living next door to them, using the bathrooms. You don't know these people, Theo, I'm telling you, they're not like us. Give them your fingers and they'll take your whole hand. And I can't stand to have them living all round me. I'll tell you again, this hotel's getting just like a bladdy shebeen. Take it from me.'

She had never spoken to him like this before. She'd be sullen, or show dumb insolence, but never such language, such shrieks. Her words must have carried to every corner of the hotel. But he'd come into her office determined to take a firm line and now he had no choice but to stick to it.

'It won't be for long,' he said evenly, 'and there won't be any trouble. If you refuse to believe that, and prefer to indulge in this silly hysterical rage of yours, then I had better leave you to it.' Without waiting for her spluttering reply, he turned and left the office.

A burst of laughter from the third-floor guest room cut short Mrs Whitney's keening soliloquy. She blanched and was silent.

Thus it was more than she could bear when she learnt the following day that Patrick had arranged with Mr Whitney to move into one of the small rooms on the third floor with his new wife, Beauty, who showed early, but unmistakable, signs of pregnancy. Mr Whitney now more than ever, was aware of a fitness in things. As Jayalakshmi had explained to him: Beauty had hidden the signs of her condition from her employers for as long as she possibly could. But it would have been only a matter of weeks before they recognised the obvious and, Beauty's sudden marriage to the ever amenable Patrick notwithstanding, sent her packing. As the hostel where Patrick boarded offered accommodation only to single men, the hotel was his last hope.

Two days later, Mrs Whitney fell ill. The doctor was called, but he was unable to diagnose the nature of her complaint, and ordered her to bed. The same night very suddenly, the air went out of her, and she died in her sleep.

Deeply shocked at the swiftness of her passing, but completely lacking in what he believed to be the natural sense of loss which he had always expected should accompany such a bereavement, indeed, feeling guilty about his inability to grieve, Mr Whitney appeared to take the death of his wife rather well.

The hotel continued to run smoothly, although a sudden influx of guests strained its facilities to the limit. If some of the guests thought it strange that none of the waiters ever seemed to go home, they put it down to staff loyalty to Mr Whitney in his time of grief, or found equally noble explanations for the courteous, efficient service they received, day and night: where there should have been chaos, they received five star attention comparable with the best of the quality hotels in the Capital.

Of course, the guests were correct when they gave the staff the credit for the smooth, professional service provided by the hotel over this unsettled period. Big David, although still confined to bed, discovered that he had some talent for figures, and devoted his time to putting the hotel's books in order. Jayalakshmi supervised the kitchen; and with the help of Anne and the part-time maids, saw to the housekeeping and to the comfort of the guests. Patrick assigned himself to general bar duties, and his reputation for amiability and aptness spread throughout the province. Soon after Mrs Whitney's death, Little David and his family, under Jayalakshmi's direction, moved to a room on the third floor. At once the most reserved and the most ambitious of the trio of waiters, Little David worked closely with Mr Whitney in deciding matters of hotel policy, coming to assume more and more of the responsibility for these decisions. He dreamt of one day taking a hotel management course in Switzerland. His happiness was extended, if that were possible, when Maria discovered that she was pregnant.

Mr Whitney spent more and more time in the hotel bar. He was often joined by Mr Stubb, and there, over glasses of brandy and water, replenished with skilful anticipation by a beaming Patrick, they would discuss in whispers their plans for the new hotel.

Arthur, or The Man Who Was Afraid of Nothing

'If you don't eat this grasshopper, then you must fight me.'

The boy's white shirt sleeve was rolled up well above his elbow and the biceps strained perceptibly in the delicate effort of keeping his fist knotted around the grasshopper to still its wrigglings without squashing it. Arthur kept his eyes on the momentous fist, blinking furiously in the sunlight that filtered sharply through the fir trees surrounding the playground. There were almost five hundred boys on the playground but they all seemed far away. Their cries were barely audible above the private singing in his ears. Occasionally, in a kind of blurry perspective, he watched a shirt float past him, white like a blister over the red dust.

He noticed that the knuckles of the boy's clenched fist were as white as he had imagined that *whitened knuckles* should be after reading about them in the books and he was conscious of feeling rather pleased, in spite of what this meant, to see his imaginative conception so exactly confirmed. Up to now he hadn't found much in books that was really true.

Still, he knew that he was going to have to eat the grasshopper. Not even the headmaster could prevent that. Despite the fact that the headmaster was hugely powerful and had shown himself capable of making his power known – to all – even to those beyond the school walls.

'I don't care if the whole of Orange Grove hears me', he would tell the boys each morning as they waited on the playground in crocodile files to be marched into their classrooms to the tune of 'The Whistler and His Dog'. The microphone which the headmaster used, as he sat behind his green venetian blinds, behind his sunglasses, gave just the right strident note of pugnacious relish to his broadcast threats.

'These are my straps,' said the headmaster to Arthur at their very first meeting, 'beware of them.' He swished a handful of them down on his desk top with a clatter.

'Yes,' said Arthur.

'Say, *Yes sir*, dear,' his mother prompted.

'We instil a sense of discipline here, which leads in time to self-discipline,' the headmaster declared, 'at least we hope that it does.' Here he gave Arthur's mother a wink. 'Each morning, the boys are assembled on the playground into crocodile files by their monitors. Then I address the school over this microphone.' He tapped the instrument with a strap. 'I say what I have to say and I don't care if the whole of Orange Grove hears me.'

After three weeks at the school, Arthur could whistle the whole of 'The Whistler and His Dog' without faltering.

Did dogs eat grasshoppers? He decided that they did not. Cats most probably did. But they would kill the grasshopper first, he felt sure of that. John the Baptist had eaten locusts and honey. Did that amount to the same thing?

He held out his hand, palm expectantly cupped. Each fir tree stood tall and erect and impartial around the playground. Several wispy clouds all resembling the boot of Italy, hung overhead. Where the strong sunlight shone on their edges they showed brilliantly white, but for the most part they looked grey and unwashed.

He found himself being pushed back against the split-pole fence. Held up by iron poles, it was rumoured to be as old as the school. Certainly, the date 1923 could be seen here and there gouged into the dark wood and that was the date in raised relief on the front wall of the old school hall. He could see one of these clumsy 1923's now out of the corner of his left eye and he clung to it because he was reassured that while he might change, it would not, and because it was so much more familiar and expected than the horny, tickling mystery in his hand. The fence still carried its erector's name on an old plaque. *Fine Fences by METALOX: Est. 1888.* The print was speckled and blotched and gave an abrasive feeling to the fingers he traced across it every day when he passed on his way home.

Arthur had never liked cauliflower. Especially not when it was served with white sauce. But he never had any option but to eat it. His father, who enjoyed it, saw to that. The trouble was that Arthur could seldom take more than a few mouthfuls without gagging and while he never actually vomited, the vocal impression that he gave of being on the point of throwing up at the table infuriated everyone who heard it, not least his mother.

'He does it out of spite,' his father would complain, throwing down his serviette at the first heaving choking sound from Arthur. His mother would sit white and silent when it happened, and say nothing.

Thus it was that Arthur evolved a new way of eating things which he thought likely to make him retch. His method was to narrow his eyes, put whatever it was into his mouth, and then with his tongue pressed firmly against his palate, chew rapidly and swallow before he actually tasted whatever he was being made to eat. The operation depended in essence upon speed and the ability attained, after some practise, of keeping every offending particle clear of his tongue and palate by holding his breath and chewing only with his molars. When he was sure it had all gone down he would take a deep breath to help him deal with the after-taste. He knew that the whole thing was more easily accomplished by holding his nose, but this, to judge from the faces around him when once he did so, excited an even greater disgust than his retching and so he never tried it again. Besides, it had a flaw because it made swallowing slower.

The fir trees did not stir. In the near complete silence Arthur could hear the other boy's starched white shirt crackle softly as he jerked himself into a new and more threatening position.

Carved into the bark of a tree parallel to the other boy's right ear was the legend: *Stuff the Boss.*

Where was the Boss now? Probably in his study polishing his straps. It was rumoured that the Boss had lined his straps with farthings for greater rigour and added impact. The bell would go any minute now and that would be the end of small break. He felt ridiculously glad now that he had decided to wait until big break to eat his sandwiches. Perhaps they would help to take the taste away. The aftertaste was the flaw in Arthur's method. Unfortunately, you couldn't keep your tongue pressed against the roof of your mouth for ever.

The incredible twitching in his clenched hand had stopped. Dead? Could he be sure? He couldn't be sure. But he knew that any movement in the mouth would destroy the method. Texture, on the other hand, didn't bother him. He imagined that it would be rather like eating a potato crisp. Or perhaps, like the satisfying crunch of a dried scab. Perhaps. He couldn't be sure. His fingers tightened into furious white fists. Dead? He'd once crushed a lizard and remembered with distaste the runnels of excrement that appeared beneath its tail. Sweat made his fingers slide a little against each other. His thighs locked as recurring shivers bombarded his back desperately braced against the warm, splintery split-pole. Sunlight honed to a knife-edge probed his eyes. He closed them. The wind stormed his resisting body with a thrust and a buffet forcing an entry, filling him with an echoing, howling void ballooning out against his ribs, his back, his bowels, bigger and bigger until he let go and it exploded out of him, ebbing away in smaller and smaller breaths until he hung frayed and empty, his thighs and buttocks dissolved and feeble, fluttering on the fence like an old rag caught on a nail.

He lay as if dead in his bed in Orange Grove. He wasn't dead yet but he would die soon. That afternoon he had crept into the lavatory at school and on an impulse rubbed one leg against the other as he had read that crickets do. The presumption of it! That night he knew he would die soon.

The following night he had an illumination. He was assured by some knowledge which it seemed he had always had that he would not die before he was exactly eighty-two years old.

He devoutly cherished both these certainties. His mother believed neither, but they alarmed her considerably; she being startled awake several nights at three o'clock by Arthur's steady hand and fixed with his unconscious eyes.

On the third morning she told her husband.

'I had to be cautious, of course,' there was a touch of blue at her lips, 'but I finally managed to worm the story out of Arthur. Now we know why he's been the way he has, you can take the necessary steps. You must please decide what's to be done. You have such a lucid mind.'

Arthur's father was a sparsely constituted man. Indeed, he was more a constituency than a man. He was put together, even down to relatively unimportant details such as the way he looked and moved, like a badly made spare part for something; something which did not exist. Although he suspected something of the sort, he clung to the belief that he was mistaken, that he would one day slide into place as snugly as a knife greets its sheath; clung desperately with the very tips of his fingers to prevent himself from sliding down into something that was perhaps nothing. His fingers were fingers like everybody else's fingers, except that they were all the same length. But that was him all over. Where others were composed of parts, he was an association of coalitions, and squared-off edges. The trouble with him was that he flowed. He fought to stay together. Where there was not coalition there was flux. Where there was flux, there was anarchy. Other people were held together by sane boundaries of planes, dimensions, distinct edges. But he could see himself stretching out into infinity like the Sahara. What on other people was merely a nose which kept its place beneath the eyes, was on him a thing which interfered with his face, pointed in two directions at once and always; its flesh lying on either cheek in anonymous collapsed piles like a rockfall. He noticed that other men contented themselves with having an idea and perhaps implementing it. To him an idea was a monstrous child that soon grew much too big for his head, burst out and slept beside him waking three times the size the next morning and sat and glared at him across the breakfast table.

This urgent need to find his place together with his terrifying ability to flow endlessly into any place whatever made Arthur's father popular with his employers. They admired in him, these employers, a quality that shone out brighter than all the others and which they took to be his conservatism. Instead, what made him seem different was an indefinable and almost boringly familiar fear that scratched and nibbled at the foundations of his being. It was a fear of nothing. Nonetheless, their mistake had got him his job in Parrot Street. His job was to keep people moving. That is, from the time they left the Department on his metaphorical left, *Influx Control*, until the time they were safely taken into the charge of the Department on his metaphorical right, *Bantu Affairs*. That the people he handled were all black women, was coincidental. Colour and sex were immaterial. His job was to ensure that while these Female Labour Units, as they were officially known, were in his line of vision, they neither strayed, slipped or stole into places, positions and jobs where as unauthorised transients they had no legal right to be.

He sat now in his office in Parrot Street and meditated on his son Arthur's latest misadventure, swivelling his chair every so often to peer down through the glass walls of his office on the crowded reception hall spread out below him. At the far end of the huge reception hall three grilled windows were set into the wall. Behind the windows sat his registration clerks. Long trestle-like benches spanned the length of the hall and they were divided into two blocks by a passageway some twenty feet wide running down the centre of the hall between the banked benches. On each bench sat fifteen to twenty women, crowded haunch to haunch, as if for warmth. In fact, the large combustion stove which burned in a corner winter and summer kept the room uncomfortably warm. Looking down on the hall from his office, the small group of women on his right hand were white. Many more women sat on his left; they were black. Silently, they faced each other across the intervening bare brown floor boards.

Directly below him, just inside the entrance, an exquisitely groomed, bewigged black woman sat at a desk. Every so often she would raise her head from the register before her and call out a number. At this signal from the receptionist a black and a white woman would get to their feet on their respective sides, join in the middle of the hall and so joined make their way up the passage to one of the grilled windows.

Here was the fountainhead which irrigated the parched soil of White suburbia – or did not irrigate it – depending on the rate of influx and egress of Female Labour Units. Arthur's father's chief function, besides ensuring that the streams from his labour pool kept flowing, was to encourage egress and to inhibit influx, one part of which, the former, he performed singularly well. So well that his ability had taken him from the caged booth of a registration clerk down in the reception hall up to the glass eyrie where he now sat with its swivel chair, heavy mahogany desk, private tea tray, strip of carpet, and shimmering electric fan that pointed out and down to repel the fumes of human sweat and fear borne upward by the hot air rising from the crowded reception hall below.

As he sat at his desk staring vacantly down on the never-ending conjunctions of colour and degree, black and white, *madam* and *girl*, forming and reforming below him, he worried about Arthur. He also worried about himself.

His bosses were showing impatience. His son had eaten a grasshopper. Neither of these things was understandable. He reasoned that his bosses were probably under pressure themselves and so they took it out on him. They urged him, forever more insistently, to try and cut down the numbers of

Female Labour Units allowed into the White Areas; to be more diligent in endorsing out those who had slipped in illegally; to keep his official quotas; to keep a more rigorous check on his clerks to see that they were not being bribed by the wealthy madams of the suburbs and to ensure that they withstood the pleas, lies, cajolery and faked doctors' certificates of the less wealthy.

'A crack in the wall means the end of the dam,' his immediate boss, the Visiting Inspector of Female Labour was fond of saying, and he had been saying so increasingly frequently of late.

But then the man had really no conception of what was involved. To endorse fifty girls out of the area today had no noticeable effect on the numbers that would be sitting patiently in the reception hall tomorrow, waiting.

The numbers grew with every passing day. At five o'clock his clerks would close their books, the great reception hall would be cleared and the last traces of the day's sweaty load vigorously swept away by the brooms and dusters of the cleaners and the floor sprinkled with disinfectant. But the ritual exorcism no longer worked, if it ever had. It seemed to him that the women never budged. That they sat there through the night incubating in the warm heat of the combustion stove, woke with the sunlight and settled again on the trestle benches in heavy, black, patient clusters to receive him without stirring when he arrived the next morning at eight o'clock.

After ten years he no longer noticed the ever-present black applicants. They were always simply *there*. A rather different kind of attention was demanded by the white madams who sat opposite him, wheedling, demanding, sometimes caressing. Wearily, he watched them re-establishing their homes, families, whole existence around this 'one girl' without whom they just, simply and absolutely, could not cope. Day after day they proved to themselves the vital dependency, their eyes widening beseechingly, inviting him to plumb in them the depths of their need. But in their voices he heard the high, indifferent notes of dull electric saws.

> My husband is sick ... is drunk ... is dead ... is syphilitic ...
> So I'll be frank ... be honest ... be straight ...
> You look like a reasonable ... a decent ... a family man ...
> I've got ten children, one blind ... defective ...
> Good servants are rare ... a gem ... a tragedy ...
> Here are certificates ... doctor's ... lawyer's ... chiropodist's ...

Certificates ... certificates ...
The voices hacked into his day. He would look dreamily down at his busy clerks behind their grilled windows, at the far end of the reception hall, and envy the remote simplicity of their routine as they dealt absorbedly with the black and white centipede crawling towards them, forever presenting its double head to be lopped off with a stroke of their ballpoint pens.

The sight always soothed him. He could feel his envy relaxing into cheerfulness. His clerks were his front line. He might not always keep to his quotas, as his bosses complained, but, by God! there wasn't an office in the country that handled efflux as rapidly as his. No other registration offices could match his disposal rate. Why, he endorsed more Female Labour Units out of the municipal area, and politely disappointed more white madams in a morning, than other offices managed in a week. He distinguished between aged, unfit, widows, women with dependant children, and the disabled, with the eye of a master. What's more, he despatched, transported, deported, repatriated, expelled, transferred, entrained and resettled these superfluous Labour Units with a smooth fluency of form and procedure that had won him the commendation of the Minister himself. He played upon the instruments of expulsion like a maestro. He walked through the jungle of towering quadruplicate forms, humped rubber stamps, tangled pass books with its fecund undergrowth of legislations and regulations and never stumbled into the snares which the white madams, or their husbands, or their lawyers, or his bosses, constantly laid in his path.

But he was not happy.

He could only be happy if his bosses who had revealed to him their ideal system, shown him the secret diastolic and systolic workings of their bureaucratic hearts, were happy too. They were not. Perhaps he could have borne their displeasure if his son Arthur had been more of a man. But he was not. If only Arthur had done something understandably bad. If he had burgled a shop or stolen from his mother's purse, or interfered with the neighbour's daughter, he felt that he could have faced it and dealt with it, and Arthur, accordingly. But for his son to have been bullied into eating a live grasshopper, and by a boy apparently half his size, was more than merely disgusting, for in some dim way which he could only vaguely perceive, it reflected on himself.

As he sat in his swivel chair at his mahogany desk, he was not alone with these thoughts. Opposite him sat the Visiting Inspector of Female Labour, drinking tea. A man whose burning sense of righteousness was evidenced in many noticeable ways; the scrupulousness with which he had his hair shaved well above his ears; the eye-riveting cleanness of his finger-nails; the careful way he modulated his anger so that it kept an even heat throughout the interview.

'We need to be men of granite,' he said.

'Oh yes.' Arthur's father had heard it all before.

'You're getting wildly above yourself,' remarked the Visiting Inspector of Female Labour calmly.

'Then it's because I'm expected to conform to influx control quotas that are wildly unrealistic. It's not my fault if the superfluous Labour Units which we endorse out of the area never arrive at the other end for resettlement. We know why they do that. They abscond, jump off the train somewhere in the veld and three days later they're back here applying for a residence permit. No, it's hardly our fault, if the Bantu Affairs Department makes a hash of things' – here he paused significantly. The Visiting Inspector was staring at the ceiling – 'nobody in the country manages a higher rate of egress than Parrot Street,' he ventured defiantly.

'Nobody in the country *needs* as high a rate as Parrot Street,' the Visiting Inspector of Female Labour replied sourly. 'Will you take credit for that too? I'm warning you, they're muttering about this in Pretoria. It's being said that Parrot Street is the weak link in the chain. They're saying that if we're not careful, Parrot Street will be the death of us. Surely you have a good idea of what will happen if uncontrolled floods of blacks stream into the cultivated white areas? Think man! You've read your Spengler, your Gibbon and your Bible!' Here he took a sip of tea. 'Think!'

Arthur's father closed his eyes and so he didn't see the Visiting Inspector stab a finger heavenward, though he heard his final, exhortatory, 'think!'

'A crack in the wall is the end of the dam,' he said without opening his eyes.

'Exactly.'

'But you can't get blood from a stone.' He stopped listening to the man's spittle-flinging expostulations, and imagined their source. He saw the lips stretch and separate and a tunnel gape immediately under the nose. Far in the tunnel's interior, upside down like a stalactite, an epiglottis beckoned above the throat's deep, black fall. In a sudden crazy whim he felt that for two pins he would leap that warning fence of tombstone teeth standing flush against the tongue and plunge down into the soft darkness buffeted by windy agitations of the pharynx. Perhaps that was his place? He opened his eyes. The Visiting Inspector of Female Labour had gone. The fan at the door wound and unwound in silver silence.

It was very quiet. Almost melodramatically quiet. He glanced over at his clerks. They sat unmoving in their cages. The light from their booths seemed to be locked into place by the arching steel grills the way the hasps of a ring hold its stone in place. He got out of his chair and walked over to the glass wall through which he could get a view of the whole reception hall. It seemed very crowded. With annoyance, he saw that there were black women sitting on the benches reserved for whites only. It was contrary to his most specific instructions. It was only when he reached the bottom of the stairs that he realised that there were no white women in the hall.

Furiously, he strode between the banked benches with their lines of patiently waiting women towards his clerks' booths. They were going to get a piece of his mind. He walked as furiously as dignity would permit, head high, a muscle dancing in his cheek, measuring off the hundred yards with a stiff-legged lofty stride. A grey haired, fading man in grey flannels, a white short-sleeved shirt, and a Wanderer's Club tie, with the unseeing gaze of an ostrich, marching through the ranks of quietly attentive women. There was an anger in his bowels that was almost pain. He stopped well before he reached the cages. What he'd taken from his office to be three men all bent over their work were, he now saw, clumsily contrived dummies, three dark jackets stuffed with paper and straw, sprawled across the desks.

He turned around. Where were his clerks? Had they arranged the dummies? He looked for the receptionist. Her desk was vacant. The waiting women watched. He knew that it was his imagination, but there seemed even more of them now. They spilled off the benches, darkening the furthest corners of the hall. Jampacked against the walls and windows they blocked out the daylight. He stood incredulous. There had never been this many before. Never in all his years in Parrot Street. Was this some trick? A joke? Something contrived by Pretoria to scare him? He remembered the menacing demeanour of the Visiting Inspector of Female Labour and the unpleasant innuendoes of their interview. He remembered falling asleep. Perhaps he was still asleep. Perhaps the Visiting Inspector of Female Labour had appeared to him in a dream. Arthur's father was not a religious man. In fact, years of contending with intractable influx quotas had the perverse effect of keeping alive his faith in a manipulable universe. He had been within sight of success so many times. The fact that the master manipulators had proved themselves to be botchers was regrettable but hardly mysterious. One had to look no further than Pretoria for the culprits. Nonetheless, he knew his Bible. Perhaps his dream interview with the Visiting Inspector of Female Labour, if it had been a dream, was a warning omen. Possibly, his clerks had been warned too, and had slunk away while he dreamt. He knew that he might still be dreaming. He ground his teeth, raging with indecision. A warning against what?

All this time he stood stock still, with his eyes blurred and the pain in his bowels growing worse. He remembered where he was. He took a breath and blinked to focus his eyes. What he saw made him sick. The stairs leading up to his office were choked with women, some standing, some lounging against the banisters, others sitting with their feet dangling over the sides. They clung to the staircase which swayed under their weight, the way a flypaper encrusted with black bodies sways from the ceiling. 'I must not panic,' he told himself, 'they can always sense panic.' But he realised that this was nonsense because the black silence around him neither knew nor cared whether he panicked or not. The women's eyes were on him. Thousands of dark eyes centred on him without seeing him. Eyes like sunflowers in an immense field adjusting to the sun. And the eyes stripped him bare.

'Ladies,' he began. It was becoming hotter, more stuffy, more crowded. No sooner was the word out of his mouth than he realised that a general address simply wouldn't work. But he knew that he must say something. Something that would stop the shuffling, scraping rustle of sounds coming from every corner of the hall and which meant that the applicants were becoming restless. Something soothing but assertive. He turned and looked at the woman on his right. She had a hard flat face. A flat face that a child draws on paper, without dimensions. A mask of a face glued to a hard little nob of a head, atop a heap of blue and red blankets.

'Now listen my girl,' he said. He put his hand on her shoulder. He was prepared to be kind but he was determined to be firm, at the same time. He took a deep breath – and then he began to scream. Incredulously, he looked at the deep gouges, the mark of teeth, the blood on his wristbone, and he screamed again. Energetically, singlemindedly, and with every fibre of his being, his head tossed back, buttocks rigid, he howled and bayed at the roof.

But the angry rustling crescendo that filled the hall was much louder than his single cracked voice. The huge fierce droning drowned it and deafened him. The air was black with wings and horns and sharp with pincers. The roof whirled and he fell. Then they began to tear at his eyes.

'O, ladies,' was all he said.

Arthur's mother had decided to give the headmaster a piece of her mind. She sent Arthur to his bedroom and then sat down to compose a very short speech. When she was happy that she had what she wanted to say off by heart, she dialled the headmaster's number. He answered promptly.

'This is Arthur's mother, Headmaster,' she told him. 'I want to inform you that one of your boys has bullied and victimised my son. The fact of the matter is that Arthur was made to eat a grasshopper,' she paused, and then shouted into the mouthpiece, 'a *live* grasshopper!'

'He must have been most terribly upset,' said the headmaster.

'I am upset, Headmaster, and so is Arthur's father, and I'm warning you that the matter will not end there,' said Arthur's mother. 'As you might have noticed, Arthur is a big boy for his age. A lot bigger, it seems, than this other creature. Now, I have told Arthur that he is to go to school tomorrow and to seek out this mongrel, this lunatic, and he is to beat him within an inch of his life!'

There was silence while Arthur's mother breathed heavily into the receiver. Then the headmaster spoke.

'Madam,' he said, 'I will tell my boys tomorrow morning at assembly as I have told them many times before – and I don't care if the whole of Orange Grove hears me – there will be no fighting in my school.'

In his bedroom, Arthur lay face down on his bed and cried. As he cried his hands flailed up and down upon the pillows, like broken wings.

Ndbele's People

Father Ndbele came from the north, and he came as a sign. His country was a desolate place, a former native reserve, remote, drought-stricken and strikingly eroded, which had been declared a self-governing new African state by the regime in Pretoria. We white people, Father Ndbele was told by Father O'Shea, his new parish priest, seemed to have found a way of disproving the old prophecy that the poor were always with us; if the poor were too much with us then we declared them independent. Into this new, poor and independent state, as was becoming customary, a go-ahead Lebanese entrepreneur flew with plans for a prodigious casino, an enormous complex created amid some ten thousand acres of virgin veld, a multi-storey concrete and glass mountain filled with gaming tables, fruit machines, cinemas, nightclubs and discothèques and surrounded by swimming pools, tennis courts, an eighteen-hole golf course and a rugby pitch. This was the course later famous among golfers who found themselves attended by troops of curious baboons, for several holes were so situated as to be indistinguishable from the enormous private game reserve well stocked with lion and elephant which lay alongside. To this great city of fun in the veld thousands of people were expected to flock for pleasures denied them at home; to play the tables, to watch banned movies and to fall into bed with pretty black hostesses.

The entrepreneur's name was Karam. A stocky, muscular,

level-eyed gangster, irritable and dark-haired, who travelled everywhere by helicopter and spoke with what he clearly imagined to be an American accent, Karam flew in to negotiate the foundation of his new casino with the young chief who was now the chief minister of the new independent, drought-stricken territory, Gabriel Shushwe, a handsome and confident young accountant who had the immediate advantage over Karam of possessing a genuine American accent picked up in the years he had followed a business administration course in Philadelphia.

He pointed out that the constitution forbade the selling of land to foreigners.

'And I should know, baby, because I wrote that damn constitution myself.'

'Maybe you lease it, then?' Karam asked.

'Sure. The constitution allows leasing of land to foreigners.'

'How about ninety-nine years?'

'I'll give you fifteen.'

'You want me to invest millions in this patch of bush in exchange for a fifteen-year lease? Come on, Chief Gabriel, give me a break.'

'Fifteen years,' repeated the chief. 'Renewable. I can't say fairer than that.'

'Such kindness – it knocks me over,' rejoined the Lebanese.

'You're welcome,' came the smiling rejoinder. 'And there will be no hidden fees, or pay-offs. In return the state will want a tooth in the proceeds.'

Karam was wary now. 'You mean a share?'

Shushwe nodded. 'Fifty per cent. Off the top.'

Karam let out an incredulous yelp. 'Off the gross? You're joking!'

'And we will have employment contracts for all my people who work for you.'

'By Jesus!' The angry Karam punched his knee painfully to help him keep his mouth shut. You didn't go into a new homeland and start abusing the chief. That was one of the first things you learned as an entrepreneur. Chief Shushwe was a greedy, grasping, jumped-up little black turd. He wanted to say that, but instead he went into his usual speech: 'You're going on the map, Chief Shushwe. A palace is going up here. There'll be everything the punter desires. From simple pleasures to sumptuous luxury. I should know,' he added confidently, 'because I got other places.' Yet traces of the anger remained though he tried to make it sound complimentary: 'By God, you got a hard nose. A real operator. A real, bloody, smart operator.'

Shushwe inclined his head graciously. 'Sure,' he said.

Father Ndbele left his dusty homeland round about the time that Karam's pleasure palace rose out of the bush and the first of the great drugged animals, elephant and rhino, began arriving in their huge wooden cages to stock the game park, and the sprinkler system was being buried beneath the rugby field. He left with a sense of heightened expectation. At the little ceremony organised to mark his departure Chief Gabriel Shushwe spoke to Ndbele as the assegai tipped with tungsten aimed at the heart of white South Africa. He pointed out that the new aim of the church to reverse their missionary role was a welcome sign of their greater understanding of the emergent black Africa, and he pointed out, too, that this reversal in church policy coincided with a very similar move among the major banks which he applauded; appointing black managers in black branches was not only sharp business practice but it had probably been instrumental in stirring the conscience of the church and he'd like to put himself on record, he told his listeners, as welcoming the willingness the powerful institutions had shown to bury their old European prejudices and turn to black Africa in a positive and co-operative spirit. Father Ndbele, Chief Shushwe said, was going out rather as Moses had done into the land of Pharaoh, he was a sign that where bankers led, churchmen might follow. The guests peered over the rims of their wine glasses at little Father Ndbele, slender, gentle, with his delicate, fluttering fingers and his large Adam's apple, full of sudden and unexpectedly quick little half-smiles that so unexpectedly brightened his dreamy features, and they thought and perhaps some of them even wished, that Father Ndbele might have been a more substantial sign.

'You're going to run into the big heat out there,' Chief Shushwe warned.

'It's my mission,' the little priest replied simply. 'I must carry the good news to the white people; they will become my people.'

'Don't bank on it,' said Shushwe.

'Give me your blessing,' Ndbele asked his chief.

'Sure.' Shushwe punched the young priest playfully on the arm. 'Go out and crucify the bastards.'

Father O'Shea, big and burly in his black cassock, a Wexford man, with a red rawboned face and prominent but very beautiful jug ears, welcomed the young black priest to his parish. The Church was reassessing, in the words of the diocesan bishop, its mission to the heart of Africa, concentrating less on converting black Africans from their far-flung pagan innocence and rather more on converting secure and white congregations from their comfortable racialism, and Father Ndbele featured as one of the shock troops in that campaign. Father Ndbele's appointment to the parish was intended to be a sign of things to come. Father O'Shea had to confess to himself, looking at the delicate young man before him, that he might have wished a rather more recognisable sign.

Despite Father O'Shea's attempts to keep his congregation together they split down the middle when Ndbele joined the parish. What no one was prepared to do was to follow Father O'Shea's line that this was a perfectly unexceptional appointment. There were those like Sam Mervyn who completely supported Ndbele's appointment and said that the time for prejudice was over and that everyone had better get used to the idea that times were changing. As a banker he had seen clear signs of it in his own business, he'd witnessed an African appointed manager of a large township branch of his bank, although this had been against his advice and to the exclusion of his own nominee, yet, as he said with a rueful smile, he'd recognised, he'd had to recognise, that times were changing. Among his supporters he listed Arthur 'Porky' Reynolds, the picture restorer, with his huge, pear-shaped face and heavy, smoky eyes, whose son had entered the seminary to become a Redemptorist, as well as Tim O'Hara, the retired jockey and old Valenti, the scrap metal merchant. On the other side was Boy Stockenstroom the builder and his tough bunch. Father O'Shea saw early how the two sides were lining up. One Saturday afternoon he strolled into the church while his priests were hearing confessions, from four until six o'clock, the penitents kneeling in the last few pews on either side of the central aisle, adjacent to the confessional boxes housing their favourite priests. When people like Sam Mervyn and his friends came they would pointedly cram the pew outside the black priest's door. Then Boy Stockenstroom and his lot began arriving, dusty in their working clothes, smelling of beer from the pub and flicking the icy holy water off their fingers, peering with deliberate, mocking scrutiny at Father Ndbele's name on the cardboard card slotted into his door, only to turn their backs contemptuously on Ndbele and his waiting penitents and move off into the opposite pew, irrespective of who happened to be hearing confession there. Stockenstroom's lot were Jeff Craskil, superintendent of the focal swimming pool (who was to be run out of town in later years for interfering with little girls), Rob Butler, the brick salesman, and the violently unpredictable Colonel Pienaar. Neither side was above hissing loudly and waving over potential recruits into their pews to swell their opposing votes. Hot looks pulsed across the aisles separating the warring camps. Father O'Shea wondered if Father Ndbele had noticed the battle lines being drawn.

Sam Mervyn's wife went further and faced Father Ndbele with a question, being a determined woman who had served in the Air Corps during the war. One of the few women to qualify as a gunner although the war had never moved far enough south in Africa to reach here, she had nonetheless achieved considerable fame in 1943 when on a single summer's afternoon shooting practice the anti-aircraft squad under her command had shot down thirteen consecutive dirigibles and her picture had appeared in all the papers.

'I don't know if you realise it, Father, but it's only fair to warn you that your appointment to our parish is seen in two very different lights. There are those, like me, who welcome it, but there are others who don't want you here. It's the old question I'm afraid.'

The little priest gave his gentle smile. 'I cannot make those distinctions. A priest must be one with his people. How else can he lead them out of bondage?'

Later, Mrs Mervyn said to her husband, with a shake of her head, 'I think he sees us as Israelites. It really is very strange.'

She did all she could to make him part of the community, inviting him on to her charity committees which organised parish jumble sales, raffles and fêtes, and it was because he'd offered his quarters as a storeroom that Ndbele acquired the great piles of old newspapers which were later to be so important to him.

The chief minister of Ndbele's independent homeland wrote an inquiring letter:

> *Dear Father,*
> *Have you civilised them yet? I'll bet not! Those people are built to the old design. The only way you'll ever fix them is to scrap the lot and start rebuilding from the ground up. Take my word for it.*
> *Yours encouragingly,*
> *Gabriel Shushwe (Chief Minister)*

Ndbele replied thanking the chief minister for his concern and saying that although he was completely at one with his people it was probably too soon to expect his people to have become one with him.

It was very shortly after this that there were delivered the two hammer blows which were to smash the last vestiges of Father O'Shea's hopes of having the black priest accepted as a normal member of the congregation. The trouble began when O'Shea placed Father Ndbele on what was known as the 'late list'. This was the stand-by roster for which priests volunteered and it meant they could be called out at any time of the day or night to administer the last rites to the dying; at least in practice, up until then, priests had volunteered but Father O'Shea was determined that the majority of these cases would be seen by the black priest. That way, he reasoned, his parishioners would come to see him merely as another priest whom they needed in this vital role as the bringer of relief and comfort and grace to the departing soul, and the prejudices against Ndbele would slowly disappear. A man who could treat you when you were dying, Father O'Shea reasoned, would surely be allowed to join the Catholic Men's Guild and the other powerful parish steering committees traditionally dominated by Boy Stockenstroom and his people. This plan had a most unforeseen and regrettable consequence. It led to the first of the two hammer blows which destroyed O'Shea's best hopes, namely death and the chemical toilet.

When the call came for extreme unction it seemed to Father O'Shea to have a singular appropriateness and it showed once again the mysterious ways in which God moved, for it represented a chance of revealing, more graphically than any sermon, that in desperate situations the human soul cries out to its priest for consolation, regardless of his skin colour.

The distraught and dishevelled caller was Jeff Craskil, Stockenstroom's willing lieutenant in the anti-Ndbele brigade, frantic with worry and lack of sleep, a biscuit-coloured duffle coat pulled hastily over his striped pyjamas which flapped showing bony ankles and black shoes with trailing laces. His mother was sinking fast and the priest would have to hurry. He had no time left to argue when he was presented with Father Ndbele carrying his little leather bag with the holy oil and sacred viaticum, though it must be said he managed through white lips to express the hope that his poor mother would not be too startled at finding what he called a 'strange priest' in the house. She was after all one of the old school, he said with a significant look at Father O'Shea, if he knew what that meant. Father O'Shea knew what it meant but chose not to reply. Instead he simply looked at his watch and Craskil fled into the night with Ndbele in tow.

The old lady lay on a great bed with a carved headboard of yellow oak in whose high polish were reflected the stacked pillows propping her and her thin grey hair. Her mouth was open and she breathed in short and sharp, tiny breaths and there was a little sweat on her lip. The doctor was packing up and told Ndbele that there was nothing more he could do, that she had had moments of lucidity throughout the evening but it was unlikely that she would say anything to him now. Jeff Craskil went with the doctor when he left the room and Ndbele closed the door and went and sat down by the bed. There was no response when he whispered her name. It was too late to hear her confession and she was in no condition to receive holy communion. Taking the little bottle of holy oil from his bag and a swab of cotton wool he began to anoint her. This was his first death and seeing old Mrs Craskil so peaceful Ndbele was relieved, there was something reassuring, almost touching, about the gentle departure. Dabbing the oil on her forehead and whispering a general absolution he was astonished to see her eyes open wide, as if his touch had revived her; clear and grey they focused on him.

Disconcerted he sat down on the chair by her side. His attempt to administer extreme unction, the viaticum, the consolation to speed the departing soul on its way, appeared to have had the opposite effect. Mrs Craskil was very much alive, indeed she appeared to be trying to sit up in the bed.

'Well Thomas – what's this I find? Sitting down on the job?' Her voice was strong, clear and demanding. A trace of holy chrism he'd left on her forehead gleamed at him. To his horror she continued to struggle up in bed until she lay propped on one elbow. 'Well, go on,' she commanded. 'Don't think because I'm sick I can't keep an eye on you.' She glared at him.

Ndbele was nonplussed, but only momentarily. Looking down he saw he was still holding the swab of cotton wool and the bottle of oil.

'Well get on with it, boy.'

Ndbele walked over to the corner, dabbed a little oil on the cotton wool and began polishing the large chest of drawers, conscious that she was watching him closely.

'And when you've finished, Thomas, I want to see my face in those drawers, shining like the sun.' With a long sigh she lay back on the pillows.

Ndbele kept his head down, concentrating on his work. He was pleased that Chief Gabriel Shushwe couldn't see him now. He was pleased no one could see him now. However, what course was open to him but to respect the wishes of the dying? He blew on the fine grain of the wood and rubbed again. The shine was coming up beautifully. He went on polishing until he was quite sure that the feeble breathing in the big bed had ceased.

Outside the room Jeff Craskil sat in a chair, head bowed, white-faced and weeping softly, his toe-caps touching beneath his pyjama trousers, the laces trailing. Beside him stood another, bigger man in electric blue flannels and a white open-necked shirt through which the chest hairs prickled like black needles. He had a red angry neck and scrubby hair, both of which he was rubbing angrily with a large square hand.

Craskil turned his brown eyes upward in a sad inquiring glance at Ndbele, who shook his head. Making an effort to control himself Craskil indicated the big man. 'This here is my mother's relation from Uitenhage. He's been travelling all night to be here before – he was devoted to her.'

The relation from Uitenhage barely glanced at Ndbele.

'Can I go in now? Can I see her?'

'Mrs Craskil has passed away,' Ndbele said softly. 'It was very peaceful. I think she was happy at the end.'

Jeff Craskil sighed deeply, he had been preparing himself for this.

'Why don't you go in and see your grannie now?' Ndbele suggested kindly to the relation from Uitenhage.

'Strictly speaking, she's not really his grannie, it's a distant relationship. But he was devoted to her,' Craskil said.

The big man went over to Craskil and began banging him on the chest. 'What's this black chappie got to do with anything?'

'He's a priest.' Craskill caught the big man's fist in his hands and patted it reassuringly. 'Perhaps we should go in and see her now.'

The relation from Uitenhage stood there in what were no doubt his best electric blue flannels and his white open-necked shirt through which even more chest hairs now pricked like black needles and out of which his red angry neck massively jutted, and leaving his fist in Craskil's grasp, he reached up with his free hand and rubbed angrily at his scrubby hair in furious confusion. 'What's there to see? She's gone. After travelling hundreds of miles to see her I arrive to find some bloody native has beaten me to it.'

'I was glad to give her what comfort I could,' Ndbele said modestly. 'The place of the priest at such times is with his people.'

The big man withdrew his fist from Craskil's consoling clasp and with it hit Ndbele in the face. 'You haven't got no people here!' cried the grief-stricken relative. 'To think she closed her eyes on that face . . .'

Craskil helped Ndbele to his feet. 'He was devoted to her. I did warn you.'

'She died peacefully. I can promise you that, sir.'

'Peacefully! I'll give you peace!' The big man hit Ndbele again in the face.

'And he's not a Catholic. That's the problem,' said Craskil.

Now this attack on Father Ndbele presented the parish priest, Father O'Shea, with considerable problems. He could not be seen to be in any way overlooking or condoning the assault on one of his priests engaged on a mission of mercy.

He interviewed Jeff Craskil and found the man distinctly unhelpful. There was the question of his relation's deep devotion to old Mrs Craskil, there was in addition the fact that he had told Ndbele that the man was regrettably not a Catholic, and perhaps most importantly there was the fact that his relation did after all come from Uitenhage and people there, he put it to Father O'Shea, were probably most unused to the sight of African men emerging from the bedrooms of cherished family members late at night. Father O'Shea rejected all of these explanations and roundly condemned the attack on one of his priests. 'A priest is God's man on earth,' he told Craskil fiercely. Craskil, angered by what seemed to him an unjustified attack, retorted that if Father believed that, Father would believe anything.

Sam Mervyn and his wife, Reynolds, O'Hara and Old Valenti announced that they would encourage Ndbele to sue the relation from Uitenhage, that they would find a lawyer and pay his costs, that this was an issue on which it was vital to take a stand. Father O'Shea found himself in a dilemma. He did not feel that he could for a moment allow anyone to believe that he thought of the attack as anything other than outrageous, stupid and impious. On the other hand he recoiled from the vision of a court case, of members of the parish, of the warring political factions parading through the witness box and, inevitably, across the back pages of the Sunday papers.

It was Ndbele himself who got Father O'Shea off the hook. He declared that on the one hand the attack by the relation from Uitenhage was a most serious assault not least because, whether Catholic or not, the man had laid violent hands on God's anointed. On the other hand, there was the question of the man's grief, and a grief-stricken man is not responsible for his actions. And certainly he had no intention whatsoever of pressing charges. In fact he rather thought he may have provoked the relation from Uitenhage. On reflection he had decided that in his behaviour on the night in question there was clearly a certain element of provocation.

Father O'Shea rubbed his forehead disbelievingly. 'You're

asking me to accept that you were in some way responsible for this primitive attack?'

Ndbele nodded.

'But how? What did you do?'

Ndbele fingered his bruised cheekbone and rolled his eyes reflectively. 'After he had hit me the first time and I got up again I think it was quite clearly in my mind as I faced him that what I intended was to turn the other cheek.'

Curiously enough when this news got around, both camps, though for their own reasons, were left equally aghast; Stockenstroom's side at the unbelievable arrogance this attitude implied, and Sam Mervyn's supporters at what they regarded as Ndbele's regrettable failure to seize this opportunity to take a white bully to court and throw the book at him. And these reactions, different though they were, had the inevitable effect of drawing, for the very first time, everyone in the parish more closely together. For the first time all of them, irrespective of their political opinions, could be seen to have reservations about Ndbele.

It was soon after this that Father O'Shea, having come secretly and regretfully to recognise Ndbele's increasingly ambivalent status in the parish, transferred him from the 'late list' to the charitable functions which abounded in the parish, those activities he and his fellow priests amongst themselves referred to as 'the social round', various committees, mostly comprising well-meaning women, which organised jumble sales, Sunday night dances, badminton, amateur dramatics, bring-and-buy sales, white elephant stalls, cake-and-candy sales. It was in this supporting role that Ndbele had first begun to solicit, collect and store in his own room considerable supplies of old newspapers. It was also about this time that, looking back, a change might have been discerned in Ndbele. For the first time instead of being merely delegated or seconded to various duties, the little priest chose to involve himself in something of his own.

He began to take an interest in the big garden, acres of wilderness, an overgrown and derelict thicket of confusion stretching from the west wall of the church to the bordering firs. He was soon a familiar sight stumping through the undergrowth, wearing an old straw hat, his cassock hitched up into his belt, his sleeves rolled well past the elbows and sweat glinting on his forehead, tending the bougainvillaea or pruning the roses. He was successful at unblocking and then carefully restocking the fish pond. He excelled at cutting back the ivy, scything the knee-high, yellow-brown grass, amidst the summer paradise of singing, stinging, buzzing insect life, uprooting the black-jacks, tidying the cypress trees and lopping dead branches from the firs.

He also worked very successfully with the women on the committees, a fact which O'Shea found pleasing though slightly disturbing. The women returned his enthusiasm by encouraging him in his work in the garden, Mrs Mervyn declaring that it was as if he found in this a way of taking root, and even Mrs Stockenstroom remarked that perhaps Father Ndbele was giving them all an object lesson in the truth that equality could not be enforced, that a man had to make his own choice, that he had to win acceptance in the community and perhaps Father Ndbele, slaving in the garden, was getting back to basics, quite literally grounding himself in their midst.

The men saw it rather differently. Sam Mervyn said quite frankly that much as the garden needed attention he couldn't see the good of a priest burying himself in his own backyard when his real function was the cure of souls, and Stockenstroom the builder, in a mood of uncharacteristic and rather menacing reflection, wondered if it was not perhaps merely that the new priest had found his own level. Father O'Shea began doubting, despite the bishop's assurances, that Ndbele represented a determination by holy mother Church to embrace its responsibilities in South Africa and this question was further clouded by another which he did not like even to admit though it knocked around in the back of his head with worrying frequency, and it was this: if indeed Ndbele was a sign, was he the precise sign Our Lord had quite intended?

The connection, the fatal connection as it proved, between

Ndbele's collection of old newspapers and his work in the garden may never have occurred had it not been for the incident at the annual Easter fête when the second of the hammer blows fell.

Ndbele was becoming increasingly noted for his work on the committees which comprised the social round, even if the popularity he was beginning to win was unavoidably confined to that minority of active women who organised these events. It was a start, the more optimistic said and even the pessimists had to agree that it was better than nothing. The annual Easter fête was held on the playing fields of a nearby school where a huge pink and white marquee was pitched, surrounded by several subsidiary tents housing a rich variety of stalls, tea and tombola, white elephant, jumble, darts and bingo. The priests came of course, everyone came: it was the premier fundraising event of the year. Ndbele had been there since early morning. He had helped to put up the tents and he had judged the homemade jams with what everybody agreed had been great delicacy and aplomb. They say he won a small bottle of shampoo on the tombola stand, lost a few pennies at darts and Craskil's young daughter had brought him a cup of tea, which everyone thought was a good omen and hinted at, some felt, a growing air of acceptance of the little black priest.

It was one of those perfect afternoons when the clean, delightful sunshine of an African autumn lay shining on the thick, rugged grass of the playing fields. Perhaps after all it was true that different races could accommodate each other, perhaps this was the beginning. Perhaps. Sadly, the hopes for better relations, hopes which had taken such a knock with the death of old Mrs Craskil, were to be blasted entirely by the affair of the chemical toilet.

Like everything else that day at the fête, the chemical toilet was inside a tent. It was a very small tent, rectangular, of faded green canvas shaped rather like a telephone kiosk and it came complete with a canvas door which was shut by clicking home the large brass press studs which ran down the edge. The builder Stockenstroom was first in the queue outside the little tent, behind him stood Sam Mervyn and behind him Jeff Craskil. The sun was dropping lower in the sky and the queue threw lengthening black shadows on the green grass, a soft crisp breeze blew and an air of serenity touched the waiting men, that curious spirit of geniality which has a way of coming up on people unexpectedly in Africa. They feel the pleasantness of the late afternoon sun on their necks, raise their eyes to a high blue heaven and feel that all they survey, all the work of their hands, has been well done. It is a feeling of togetherness, of camaraderie, which leads respectable middleaged women to take off their shoes in public places and sit down on the grass and takes men from silent reflection, scuffing a toe absentmindedly in the turf, to rowdy sessions in hotel bars in the first glow of sunset. The setting sun is an event in Africa. Sundown unlocks the doors. The sun goes out like a lion and in the faint glow remaining an inexplicable and yet somehow comforting pride springs up in the hearts of white people particularly, leading women to gossip and men to brood and everyone thereafter to the drinks trolley and the hotel bar and the cocktail cabinet there to set the seal on their togetherness before the night closes in.

This mood of geniality was upon Stockenstroom who stood like a sentry, his feet slightly apart, his arms behind his back, shifting his weight from one foot to the other, patiently waiting. And he was very patient. He pointed out to Sam Mervyn, to whom he had not been talking for some weeks, that some wag had gone and chalked 'Please knock' on the canvas door. They both laughed and Mervyn turned and told Jeff Craskil. And eventually Stockenstroom at Sam Mervyn's urging politely asked the occupant of the toilet to hurry things along. The voice that replied in clear, unemotional terms shocked the waiting men, it was so unexpected. In a voice much louder than was needed to carry through the thin canvas Ndbele insisted that people would simply have to wait until he was finished. To his credit, Stockenstroom did as he was told. He waited, gouging at the back of his neck furiously with his stubby fingers, but waiting none the less. Mervyn, who was so very embarrassed, as he told his wife later, he didn't know where to put his face, whistled tunelessly. Craskil openly sneered. A few minutes later Stockenstroom, making an effort to keep his voice under control, once again asked the occupant of the tent to get a move on. The queue recoiled when the voice declared it impossible to hurry a call of nature. Deep and low somewhere inside him a reverberating note, or perhaps a croak so low, so frog-like, rose up in the builder and bubbled from his lips.

'I'll give you a call of nature!' he shrieked and opening his big arms he ran at the tent as if to embrace it, dragged it off its four wooden feet in his great bear hug and tossed it aside. 'When I say out, I mean out! You cheeky black devil!'

The tent toilet demolished at a stroke lay in a jumble of struts and canvas and there presented to the sight of the whole world was a spectacle which, as Father O'Shea said afterwards, was to cause scandal, humiliation and deep anguish to Father Ndbele himself and to all who saw it, and it is doubtful that there was anyone on that field who didn't see it. A spectacle at once brutal and farcical, the sight of Father Ndbele, with his cassock hitched to his waist and underpants around his ankles, sitting on the chemical toilet in the middle of the fête. A woman screamed, several children cried, Stockenstroom simply stood there smacking his hands together in a workmanlike way, Sam Mervyn turned his back, even Craskil stared at the passing crowd. Only Ndbele moved, in a fluid movement he reached down and then stood, his cassock safely in place swung at his ankles; his composure was astonishing and the few who could bring themselves to watch said he left the ground with the casual, natural air they found eerie and disturbing. Stockenstroom, of course, tried to say later that he would have behaved in the same way whoever it had been in the toilet, to anyone who had spoken to him in that fashion. But he wasn't believed and Father O'Shea ordered him off the church premises, removed him from his committees, struck him from the parish roll. But the damage was done.

Reaction in the parish was strange and not at all what O'Shea had expected. He got the impression, in fact he got the distinct impression, that while everybody had been extremely embarrassed by what had happened at the fête, nobody really seemed to feel that what Stockenstroom had done was reprehensible; to his alarm he sensed that people thought it was understandable and in fact if anyone was to blame for the incident it had been Ndbele, who by allowing himself to be exposed in the way he had been shattered the mood of golden geniality in which the day was ending. People held it against him, there was no doubt of that, it was almost as if they felt that he had been responsible for the attack and the builder Stockenstroom merely his unwitting victim.

Ndbele's humiliating appearance had disturbed the afternoon, it had offended the guests and his eerily dignified exit seemed positively to have enraged all who had seen it. Mrs Ada Stockenstroom's comment was typical: 'It's being a native that does it. You know what I mean.' At this point she would look hard at her hearers. 'It's being a native,' she would add again. She had their attention and was certain of their understanding. 'It's being used to being in the veld. They can just come and go there. They use the grass. For them it's natural.'

Father Ndbele returned to his garden. Parish work was no longer an issue for him. He was off the late list, he was off the social round and he spent a great deal of time carrying large white enamel basins of water into his bedroom. Father O'Shea said nothing, he was merely grateful that Ndbele seemed so fully occupied. Besides he could think of nothing to say.

One morning the reasons for the work Ndbele was doing in his room became apparent; the first of the figures appeared in the garden. It stood beneath an olive tree and was discovered by some altar boys on their way to serve the early morning mass. He was a policeman. He stood on one leg beneath the olive tree, his uniform was perfect in every detail, the peaked khaki cap, the khaki shorts, the Sam Browne over the smart russet tunic, the belt, the revolver in its holster and the handcuffs gleaming beside the truncheon dangling from its hip thong, thick brown woollen socks and the brown shoes with toe-caps boned and gleaming, though slightly misty with the early morning condensation, a pirouetting figure, one leg thrown out behind it, hands reaching into the air, head tilted back and the shadow from the cap peak shortening as the sun rose on the pallid papier-mâché features, carefully modelled and hand painted, a policeman rearing on one leg and reaching out his arms in the early morning sunshine, the first of Ndbele's people. The next morning a second figure appeared, correct in every detail from cap to toe and linking his arm in his fellow's, the pair flung their heads and feet and arms in a spirited, high-kicking dance.

The dancing policemen were the first of a set of monumental figures which were soon to occupy every corner of the garden. There followed these others: Angels Digging, a winged working party who had already scooped away in the night a great hollow of earth or a swimming pool or a ditch or even perhaps a grave, and now stood leaning on their spades and contemplating their handiwork, their great wings arching behind them, the papier-mâché thickly sprinkled with gold glitter. A working party of six. Next came the Dying Priest Attended by a Child who lay on a stretcher of twigs beneath an old army-issue blanket. His hands folded piously on his chest, the face white and staring, perhaps he was already dead, perhaps he did not see the child who had stopped beside him, holding a hoop and stick, the hoop an old bicycle wheel, the sort you saw small children driving with long wire whips in any African village, and was clearly intended as some reference to the Christ child. The priest's hair had been contrived with strips of old brown sacking and had a coarse and desperate look to it and it was with a terrible shock that Father O'Shea recognised that the features were modelled on his own. A moment's inspection showed him that the two dancing policemen had the faces of Stockenstroom and Sam Mervyn, Jeff Craskil was to be found among the angels digging as was the effigy of old Colonel Pienaar.

It did not take long thereafter to realise that what Ndbele was doing with his figures was to replace in so far as that was possible the entire parish with the population in his garden. Each day there was something new, Three Apostles Racing, Christ Wrestling a Lion in which a huge naked Christ with the face of the bishop wrestled an ungainly and rather lumpy lion. Ndbele never aimed at close realism, except in the modelling of the faces which was astonishingly done, but for the rest he aimed for force and movement, modelling his undependable and inflexible chosen medium of papier-mâché onto frames of compressed chicken wire. His last great work, a tableau of no less than sixteen figures, the Virgin Attended by her Golfers, took him almost three months to build and showed the Virgin upon a rock, rather reminiscent of the Little Mermaid, receiving a deputation of golfers, the first of whom kneels before her presenting a symbolic putter while the other golfers bring up the rear, tired and travel-stained, evidently after a long pilgrimage. The Virgin's face was that of Mrs Mervyn.

Ndbele wrote to his chief about this time:

> *Esteemed Sir,*
> *My prayers have been answered. Praise be the Lord. He has allowed his servant to come among His people at last! My ambition is to lead them out of the bondage in which I have found them, to lead them home to the land of their Fathers. Pray for me, Beloved Chief. Ask that my prayers are answered.*

Father O'Shea asked him, 'Are these your people?'

'Your own lips have said it.' Ndbele held up two fingers pressed tightly together. 'Bone of my bone, blood of my blood. I will not allow one hair of their heads to be harmed.'

Father O'Shea nodded, he seemed to approve of these

sentiments. 'Well in that case what are you going to do when it rains?'

The rain of course played havoc with the figures, they dissolved, they floated, old headlines appeared on their foreheads. Father Ndbele was almost equal to the task and he began building shelters, using any material he could find, old cardboard boxes, corrugated iron, plastic sheeting; he built lean-to's, porticos, alcoves, grottoes and tents to house his people and to keep them from the rain. Before long it seemed as if an entire shanty town had sprung up beside the quiet west wall of the church.

Something had to be done. This was a sad necessity, or perhaps a kindness. Some of the women, reminded of their cordial relations with Father Ndbele, suggested that it was clear that things simply could not go on, that the church now stood beside a slum, a township, a location full of strangely pallid natives, sleeping, standing, dancing, living and dying in shanties and lean-to's.

The attention of the municipal planning department might be drawn, it was suggested, to the obvious contravention of the zoning laws, the building regulations and the environmental provisions for the neighbourhood. However, this presented difficulties because the order, if the order was to be made against a new town, must demand the removal of Ndbele's shanties without in any way threatening the rest of church property and this was always a very delicate matter since the Catholic Church existed uneasily beneath the hostile scrutiny of a Calvinist Nationalist government opposed to the Church of Rome, commonly referred to as the Roman Danger. Once the authorities had been appealed to, the danger was, O'Shea knew, that he might find himself facing an artillery barrage fired by a government gunner who might not be unhappy at the thought of knocking out more acres of church property than simply the little patch populated by Ndbele's people. It was not even certain that the government inspectors could be expected to act at all, since they may have preferred to sit back and enjoy Father O'Shea's discomfort and his bishop's dismay at the way in which their plans had gone awry. If the appropriate authorities were to be approached, they must be diplomatically sounded out as to ways in which the business could be accomplished, how the necessary injunction was to be shaped, and then aimed so as to hit only that excrescence of canvas, cardboard, cheap matchwood and old sacking which now disfigured the formerly fair west wall of the parish church, occupying what had been the garden stretching from the box hedge to the fir trees marking the border, a pleasant if rather bedraggled spot before it had been colonised or, as some said, squatted, by the rag-tag assembly of the pious and profane creatures who had become known as Ndbele's people.

Father O'Shea called a meeting of the parish council knowing as he did so what their answer was likely to be and so felt little surprise and a keen regret when they told him that the only man with the necessary connections among municipal planning officials and the know-how of the building trade as well as the right political credentials was the builder Stockenstroom; even the Mervyns with their liberal attachments felt the undeniable logic of this. Jeff Craskil announced himself as ready to act as intermediary between the council and its former chairman and said firmly that he knew old Stockenstroom was far too decent a chap to bear any grudges.

Stockenstroom responded promptly to the suggestion that he approach the municipality and in a letter to Father O'Shea said that the job was a difficult one and one which would require him to bring all his influence to bear on his friends in the Planning Department, but declaring himself warmed by the confidence of the parish council and promising to do whatever he could to help, particularly in view of what he liked to think of as his long association with the council. The significance of these last words was not lost on the committee. The job was to be done on the clear understanding that if successful Stockenstroom was to find himself gratefully reinstated as a full member of the congregation, his reward would be a return to the fold. Jeff

Craskil was heard to remark that he understood now why there was more joy in heaven over the single sheep that is lost and found than over the ninety-nine that had been saved all along. Sam Mervyn retorted that he did not see the comparison at all and that Stockenstroom, in his opinion, was more wolf than sheep, and Father O'Shea moved quickly to hush this bickering.

He telephoned Chief Shushwe to prepare him for things to come: 'We thought, that is the bishop and I, that a visit home might be in order. We think it may help.'

'Help who?' The chief was brusque. 'I need a priest here like I need rabies. He went over to you guys because we thought you needed help. He was supposed to spread a little light among the heathen. Mind you I thought it was a mistake at the time. You guys are damned incorrigible, there's no curing you. But the little fellow is so enthusiastic. He is better than you deserve and you know it. I just hope you treated him decently. What's he going to do back in the bush all alone? Got no fancy church here.'

'He is not exactly alone.'

The chief shrieked. 'Not alone? You mean he's got company? You've got to be crazy, Father, have you any idea where I'm speaking from? My so-called independent country is a denuded, eroded, poverty-stricken dustbowl. Nothing much grows here, nothing much lives, and very few of us eat, and you're planning to send Ndbele back here with a party?'

'It is not so much of a party as a following.'

'What does it matter? It's still mouths and they will want feeding.'

'I think, Chief Shushwe, you will find these people far from demanding.'

'How did he get these people? Is he some sort of a guru where you live – little Ndbele? Where do they come from?'

'They sort of sprang up,' O'Shea said uneasily.

'Jesus, what do you mean? Has the boy been breeding in captivity?'

'We will lay on a form of transport, rely on us,' O'Shea promised desperately and hung up.

Ndbele stared at the injunction tightly packed with numbered regulations and decrees forbidding the erection of unscheduled, unplanned, illegal dwellings, domiciles, cottages, garages, mobile homes, car ports and all other forms of walled and/or roofed habitation . . .

'What does this mean?' he appealed to O'Shea.

'It has nothing to do with the Church. I am very sorry. The government say they will come with bulldozers and break all of your people.'

The little priest stood erect. 'Then I will lie down in the path of the bulldozers. People have done so before. The government are always coming with their bulldozers, we are not afraid.'

'Then you must know that the government and its bulldozers always win. They will lay flat this place and all your people and then will pack up the pieces and throw them on the rubbish heap.'

The little black priest's agonised silence testified to the truth of these remarks.

O'Shea thrust home the advantage. 'But, on the other hand, if they were to be taken to a place of safety . . .'

Ndbele raised anxious eyes. 'You know of such a place?'

O'Shea included his head. 'The homeland. The land of your fathers.'

'That is possible, but it would not be home to my people.'

'Not home, but a place to rest for a while. A place for them to lay their heads.'

Ndbele swung and faced north and stared with narrowed eyes at the distant horizon. After a long moment he said, 'It would be a refuge. It might seem a wilderness but at least they will be safe for a time. They could gather their strength for the journey into the land promised.' He wheeled suddenly on O'Shea. 'You would not try to stop us leaving?'

Father O'Shea smiled gently. 'Stop you? Why should I stop you? I am not Pharaoh. No, I shall not stop you. In fact I intend to arrange your transport.'

The day on which Ndbele and his people departed the parish was long remembered. Everyone turned up with the exception of Stockenstroom who, it was generally agreed, at his moment of triumph showed surprising tact in staying away.

The transport arrived promptly, three one-ton lorries, leased with parish funds from Moosa who hawked fruit and vegetables around the neighbourhood, rapidly rusting old lorries with open sides, and each with its scaffolding of steel poles on which from Monday to Saturday were hung Moosa's fruit and vegetables and sheaves of brown paper packets pierced on brass hooks now sliding musically along the rails at the slightest touch.

Everybody pitched in with a will that day. Supervised by Father O'Shea in a floppy khaki hat with a green brim, they rallied around the frantic figure of Ndbele whose energy was astounding, who was everywhere at once, admonishing, cajoling, thanking his helpers, whispering to his people, tenderly seeing to their comfort and welfare, as they were one by one taken from the garden and loaded aboard the lorries. The three Indian drivers were bossed by a rather haughty youth, a cousin of Moosa called Farum, and none of them lent a hand but instead sat on the bumper of the leading lorry, in what shade they could find, and told long vivacious stories to each other interspersed with peals of high-pitched laughter.

The figures presented many problems and it was hot and delicate work lifting them over the tail gates and lashing them gently and firmly into place using the overhead rails and their jingling hooks for extra security. The policemen presented a particularly awkward problem with their flinging limbs for it was difficult to know how they could be secured without running the risk of a sudden jolt tearing off an arm or a leg. Eventually Mrs Mervyn suggested that they might be lashed together for added support and so they were secured, waist to waist first, and then tied to the corner posts. The dying priest had a tendency to slide about since Ndbele insisted that the old man was too ill to leave his bed and must be laid flat. Bracing him seemed impossible until Craskil, who had once been in the navy, hit on a brilliant solution and fashioned a hammock from an old blanket, and with this they slung the priest from the top bars of the lorry like a sleeping sailor. The Digging Angels filled almost the entire lorry themselves because of the great expanse of their feathery wings which flaked easily and so they had to be laid face down and all one saw of them from the road were the tips of their wings, quivering feathers shaking like a field full of shuttlecocks in the breeze. Lastly the houses, homes, lean-to's and shanties had also to be carefully taken down, numbered and stacked. It was late afternoon before the job was complete, the child with his hoop was now in place, the makeshift clubs borne by the golfers who tended the Virgin had been collected, numbered and wrapped in sacking. The garden was at last empty, the lorries loaded and the convoy ready to roll. The driver, Guram, heaved himself up into the driving seat of the leading vehicle. Ndbele clambered up onto a pile of corrugated iron on the last lorry, Craskil banged the leading lorry on the tail gate and then to a cheer of farewells Ndbele's people set off on the long road north. The last glimpse Father O'Shea and his little band of helpers had of the convoy was of the dancing policemen, lashed trunk to trunk, oddly, eerily, intimately interwoven, swinging in their tight, roped embrace and then the tiny figure of Father Ndbele perched on his pile of corrugated iron with his knees drawn up to his chin and his face pointed to the north.

Chief Gabriel Shushwe sat in his office in a beehive-shaped building which echoed the style of the native huts outside but in his case was built of a bright and scratchy yellow-faced brick. Through the windows he could see the three lorries piled with their improbable cargo, and the three Indian drivers sitting on the front bumper. Ndbele stood before him looking around with big eyes.

'Okay, baby,' Shushwe commanded, 'spill.' With growing impatience he watched Ndbele glancing around his office, saw him staring at the huge teak desk and the armchairs, at the venetian blinds covering the windows, at the red baked earth beyond the blinds and the scruffy, dusty little fowls darting about, the swollen-bellied children in the doorways of the mud huts. Chief Gabriel felt a pang of something he hoped wasn't guilt. 'Don't knock it until you've tried it, right?' he instructed the priest. 'We're not here to talk about my position anyway. What did I send you out into the white world for, if not to teach those bastards a lesson? You were my assegai, remember? Tipped with tungsten. I expected you to punish them, to make them suffer. I wasn't sure if you'd manage it, mind you, but that was the general idea. I did not expect you to turn up here one day with a lorryload of ghouls tied up with ropes and three Asian drivers. God dammit, man, you were sent out there to throw pepper into the eyes of the white racists, not to start your own tribe!'

Ndbele gave him a proud look. 'A man cannot choose his own destiny.'

Gabriel stared out of the window and thought of America, of his happy days at Penn State University. Sunlight on the Delaware. A girl called Sheena. Outside his window he saw a woman, baby strapped on her back, tending a row of mealies, hacking the iron ground with an old hoe. 'You're telling me, boy,' he said feelingly.

Chief Gabriel slept on the problem. But in the praise-songs of his tribe it is related that that night he dreamed, though this was never confirmed. However, in the morning he spoke urgently to Ndbele who had slept the night on the back of a lorry and he said nothing at all to the three Indian drivers who were by this time angry, hungry and impatient. His words were prophetic: 'This is thin country, there's no place for you here.'

When Ndbele asked where he should go, the chief's reply was to climb up into the cab of the leading lorry and to order Guram to drive.

They drove along the new, metalled road leading to the casino, they drove through the huge car parks where the sun shone liquid on a thousand Japanese sedans and they drove through the serried ranks of tourist buses, past the tennis courts, past the great gate with its motif of animal horns marking the entrance to the game reserve and stopped in front of the great glass doors that led into the foyer of the new casino.

Chief Gabriel Shushwe's first words to the entrepreneur Karam are legend: 'Be of good cheer, baby,' he said, 'a holy man has come amongst you.'

Karam swore. He tore his shirt in his rage. It did no good.

The full-sized rugby field was chosen as the best site. The pavilion and sprinkler system ensured that there would be a supply of running water. Soon that green and luxuriant patch of grass between the touch-lines took on a more homely aspect as Ndbele began rebuilding the shelters.

'It came to me,' Chief Shushwe told Karam, 'that what this boy needed was a promised land and you're the nearest thing to it.'

'I won't support these people,' Karam warned.

'They're your employees now. On contract,' Shushwe warned.

'Jesus wept!' the Lebanese yelled.

'And you better cut out that sort of talk right now. They're holy.'

Karam ripped aside the tattered shred of his shirt to expose his chest. 'Cut my heart out while you're about it. Drink my blood!'

'I don't want nothing myself,' Shushwe said seriously, 'but if you've got any morsels you could spare I'm sure Father Ndbele would be damn grateful.'

Ndbele showed no gratitude to the entrepreneur in the Sunday sermons he preached to his people comparing him to a modern pharaoh holding his tribe in bondage, this to the great amusement of the curious gamblers, who as news spread would wander down from the casino for a breath of fresh air, marvel at the dignity of the tribe camped among the bits of tarpaulin, canvas, flapping blankets and corrugated iron and inspect with growing awe the figures ranged across the rugby field: dancing policemen and dying priest, digging angels and the Virgin's faithful golfers and all the holy company of Ndbele's people, now grown to a small city full of many more strange white folk, apostles with microscopes, Magdalene laughing and a St Paul, who had the face of the relation from Uitenhage, cycling. And although Ndbele might have charged something for this casual viewing he never did so; all he expected in return for the guided tours he offered and his free sermons, was a sympathetic ear into which he would pour with icy and sardonic range the story of how his people had been dispossessed and driven from their land, how they had been forced into exile and how they would endure and one day return. 'Return,' he said, lifting his fist above his head, 'driving all before them.'

On the Frontier

Maxie Meyerson ran a chemist's shop on what began as the far edge of town. He'd gone there soon after completing his pharmacy course at College, ten years earlier. He'd chosen this most unlikely suburb because it was raw bush, still practically frontier, and on the frontier a man could earn his whack and he hoped to earn a very big whack indeed. With the small inheritance his father left him he bought the shop, had his name painted, along with his pharmacy degree, on the lintel in wavy white letters and he stocked up.

Meyerson had been very influenced by his father in his decision to live rough but free. On the frontier a man could do anything, Papa Meyerson said, and in Africa, new Africa, such things were possible, even for Peruvians. His father and mother had come to the goldfields of the Transvaal from Poland before the turn of the century when they were still children. They had met and married in Johannesburg where Meyerson's father worked down the mines. They were among those lower-class Jews who had belonged to the Polish Russian Union, and hence the contemptuously inaccurate description of them as 'Peruvians', poor immigrants who worked hard for the big mining bosses, sometimes Peruvians turned Anglican, who appreciated in these Europeans their useful urge to work until they dropped, however menial the role, however poor the pay. When too much dust got into Papa Meyerson's lungs and he quit, his wife Friedle found a job as concierge of a tall, damp, flaking block of flats in the centre of town. When Friedle died old Meyerson took over and dealt with the clamorous tenants, saw to the great hissing patched boiler in the basement and oversaw the fitful energies of the black houseboys who lived in concrete barracks among the chimneys up on the roof of the block. He hired them, fired them, dampened down their continual drinks parties and helped to carry out the corpses after the traditional Saturday night parties with their traditional stabbings. As young Maxie lay in his bed he would often hear the screams. The flats were old and dark, and the cooking smells, the cabbage and the onions, had impregnated the woodwork which, in all the flats, was painted a dark green. The walls and metalwork were covered in a heavy, shiny grey.

'When you get big, boy, don't you go and do what I did – don't you go and sell yourself to some fat boss. The people who came from Poland, like your mother and me – know what they did, they came away from the ghetto so as they wouldn't be murdered? Thanks very much. You think that's pretty smart? Don't you believe it, sonny. We left there to stop being murdered and came here to find ourselves committing suicide. Don't go working for nobody, Maxie. You go into business for yourself. This is Africa. Being born Polish and stupid, what we didn't know could fill libraries. But you can do it. You can do anything you like here. It's frontier.'

His father never lived to see the shop Maxie bought with his small sum and a bank loan, just three weeks after completing his pharmaceutical studies. But the old man had left him in no doubt of his belief that he would eventually make it and the purchase of the shop on the furthermost edge of the city was a source of enormous pride to Maxie. When he moved in, it was true to say that he was quite literally confronted by bare veld. There was no other chemist's shop for miles.

But Maxie looked the other way for a moment and progress caught up. Soon ditches and foundations were being dug, trees cleared, and houses were going up and all the red dust was a considerable irritation to Meyerson in his early years because he found it almost impossible to keep his windows clean and he was continually dusting his shelves. When the construction was at last finished he found himself in possession of a chemist's shop right in the middle of an undistinguished white suburb where the mothers sent their kids in for magnesia and aspirins and bicarb, for patented nerve pills, and for laudanum-laced potions with Dutch names used for knocking out the baby when he wouldn't sleep, and liver pills. But business was business and the prescriptions multiplied as the young wives who moved to the neighbourhood became mothers and needed drugs. Prescriptions paid his bills in the early years when his counter trade ran at a loss and the kids came in barefoot and shaven-headed and stole cough-drops and glucose tablets if he dared to put them on his glass shelves in front of the till. They wrestled with each other, two, three, and sometimes four of them crammed onto the big green scales by the door which gave your weight for a penny, and he'd rush at them and bowl them out onto the street. But business grew, along with the families it served, and he prospered and he thought sometimes with honest pleasure of the pride his father would have felt.

The natives were something of a problem. He wouldn't turn them away from his store: they were customers like anyone else, and when they had money and he had the goods, why shouldn't he serve them? And he wouldn't fence off his shop into two halves; Meyerson was no racist. On the other hand he couldn't allow his white customers to be swamped by black men and women off the streets who came in to buy cheap plastic jewellery, or bleaches for their skin, or hair straighteners, or hairpins, or lipsticks. So he instituted a rule that only one African was allowed in at a time. It was an unwritten rule and by and large it was unspoken too, but it was understood throughout the servants' quarters in the backyards of the new houses and it was rare that Meyerson had to ask the black customers to leave the shop and wait in line outside the glass doors.

Meyerson, small, dark, prematurely balding in his late twenties, but full of energy with an incisive, abrupt manner to him, worked very hard, worked, as his father would have said, like a European, living in the two rooms above the shop, cooking and cleaning for himself, slaving for the ten years that it took to repay the loan to the bank. He did not go to the cinema. For recreation he walked. At night he read the trade papers, then went to bed. He didn't like that loan, it smacked of working for a boss, though he knew of course that it was very different; a lot of businessmen took money from the bank, that's what banks were there for. His friend Michaelis, a fashion buyer, urged him to keep on the loan, saying it was cheaper to service the debt than to eat into his capital in repayments, but Meyerson persisted. The bank wasn't a boss but it felt like one, and so he paid back the debt for his father's sake.

When he paid off the debt, Meyerson expected at last to make his packet. In truth his profits had been growing; this was due in large part to what he called his 'lines'. For Meyerson did not make his money from his prescription charges, or his patent medicines, or his counter trade. He made it by isolating and then promoting some new line. He got advice about the latest gimmick in the trade from his friend Michaelis, when they met once a month for their lunch in the Railway Hotel. Over that invariable roast beef, Michaelis would tell Meyerson what was on the up and up, what women were after just then. Meyerson handled his promotions with the same energy and enthusiasm which he brought to everything else. One month it would be a new permanent wave. He would hire a hairdresser and a model, set up a chair right there in his shop and demonstrate to his customers the wonderful setting qualities of this new product on which he was making a special offer, for one week only, whilst stocks lasted, and the hairdresser would wash and set the model's hair right there in the shop in front of a small audience of enthusiastic housewives from the suburb, while out on the pavement a group of curious and slightly disbelieving Africans would watch with big eyes through the window. In this way, Meyerson promoted electric hair rollers, herbal cosmetics, the latest aids in chiropody for those with troubled feet, and always with demonstrations, always with expert advice, always with special offers whilst stocks lasted. The interest this provoked amongst his white customers inside, and his black customers outside, the shop, increased as time went by. It was amongst one of these excited groups of bewitched Africans that Meyerson first noticed the albino.

He was tall, around twenty, in an old grey felt hat with its broken brim pulled down over his ears and a pair of sunglasses with bright green plastic frames. He was a thin boy and his clothes were old, probably cast-offs, a dirty green sports coat and threadbare, flapping grey flannels short enough to show he wore no socks. It was strange to see this pale, tattered creature prancing around on the cat-walk in his dirty tennis shoes, talking and laughing with the other Africans. He seemed to speak their language perfectly. He'd probably been raised as one of them, Meyerson reflected. It was bad being neither one thing nor the other, despised by every colour in the country, worse even than being a Peruvian.

Then one day the albino walked into the shop and applied for a job. Meyerson was too flustered for a moment to know what to say. As if he thought it might help his request by showing what good manners he had, the albino reached up and took off his old grey felt hat and held it clasped in both hands in front of him. His hair was milky white through which the scalp showed pinkly. The overhead neon lighting danced in his dark glasses with their bright green frames and he shuffled a foot as he waited for Meyerson's response.

He was genuinely taken aback, he had never thought of anybody else doing this work; he ran a shop and what the shop took to run he did. That's all there was to it. He'd never considered anybody else doing the work for him.

'I can sort the stock,' the albino said, 'or I can keep the place clean and neat. I'll do anything. It's not easy for people like me. We're monsters from the bush.' The dark glasses with their hideous green frames flashed at him. 'Give me a break, Mr Meyerson.'

'What's your name?' the chemist asked, to buy time.

'Gus.'

'Well, Gus, I'm sorry, but I don't have no work. This is a one-man show.'

'I could be a delivery boy.'

'I don't deliver,' said the chemist.

'You could if you had me.'

A customer came into the shop. It was Avril Boersma. She had a bad heart and had come to collect her prescription he'd filled that morning. Her large white legs in their tiny black pumps stomped across the floor. She stared the albino up and down with an inscrutable expression. Meyerson felt deeply embarrassed. Avril Boersma was an important woman: her late husband had been a colonel in the army, and she was prominent in the local school board of governors besides being a woman who attended all his demonstrations of his new lines and bought copiously the products on offer. She leaned her marbled, fleshy forearms on the glass counter and breathed heavily, keeping her eyes on the albino.

'I don't need anybody,' Meyerson snapped. 'Nobody. Now scat.'

'It don't pay to be out in the wild on your own. Think about it.' The albino replaced his hat, pulling it over his ears carefully, and then he turned and walked with great dignity and without looking back, out of the door.

Meyerson shrugged his shoulders. 'An albino.'

'I seen him around, the white nightmare. That's what you get from marriage across the colour lines, Mr Meyerson, mark my words.'

'I reckon it goes hard for people like him. Strangers everywhere.'

Mrs Boersma snorted. 'We don't need things like that here. This is a respectable neighbourhood. What's he want, Mr Meyerson – begging, was it?'

'He wanted to help in the shop.'

Incredulity rippled across her forehead. 'Help you may need, Mr Meyerson, but that walking warning for his father's sins you can do without.'

The subject of assistance came up again when Michaelis gave him advance notice of a new product soon due on the market. 'A sort of home-tanning kit. It's catching on really big in Europe now, they say, and you really can't tell it from the real thing providing you apply it properly. Smart packaging with choice of roll-on or spray. Secret formula contains a super bronzing agent. It's perfect for your offer of the week. Order in advance and I can get you a good discount, it'd make a beautiful in-store demo, not so?'

Meyerson said he thought it would, only the special offers cost a lot of effort.

Michaelis patted his friend on the shoulder. 'Sure. You're doing the counter at your place – right? And the books, taking the stock, running the prescriptions, and I'll bet doing the deliveries too.'

'We don't do deliveries,' Meyerson said.

Michaelis spooned horseradish onto his roast beef. 'OK, so you're sweeping out, I'll bet. Wise up, Maxie, get in some help.'

The chemist replied that while he could manage himself he preferred it. 'If I took someone on I'd feel I owed him. I don't want to feel beholden to anyone.'

'So don't behold – *employ*,' the fashion buyer retorted.

Without asking his friend he sent along the girl. Her name was Maureen Gwass. She'd come to him wanting to be a fashion model but she was dumpy, her ankles were too thick, and so he was passing her on to his old friend who had a good thing going in the cosmetic and styling lines and maybe could use her.

Meyerson stared. When she turned he saw her ankles were rather thick, the calves golden in her best sheer stockings. Then she was dumpy, true, but shapely. And she smiled at him, sweet and full. Her complexion was bright and clear and the auburn hair lay thickly on her shoulders and she thanked him so profusely for giving her 'a leg up in life' that he hadn't the heart to tell her that he didn't need any help.

She began work the next day and he soon felt that she had changed his life: she wore a white coat and quite of her own accord turned up one morning with large letters embroidered in blue across the shoulders: 'Meyerson's Pharmacy'. She made him tea, she swept out the shop, she tidied the stock-room, she watched with fascinated awe when he dispensed medicines. 'You are a brainy man, Mr Meyerson. I wish I had half of your brain.' Meyerson, delighted with the attention he was getting for the first time in his life, repaid her by giving her little gifts, the small sample bottles of perfume which the travelling salesmen left, trial lipsticks and sachets of shampoo. It was the demonstrations, however, into which Maureen entered with real flair and conviction. There was no longer any need to hire models; it was Maureen's hair that was permed with the week's cut-price offer, Maureen's lips that were painted, Maureen's nails that were varnished. The girl basked under this preening and her delight infused Meyerson with a great sense of pleasure and accomplishment. Soon, he realized, he was desperately in love with her. As for Maureen, her happiness increased by the day. Principally, he saw, because she imagined her small modelling successes were leading her slowly but surely to the stage or the cinema or the television screen, or to whatever glittering venue she had dreamt would one day be her natural place. Meyerson saw the folly of this but said nothing, merely being happy that she was happy.

One evening when Maureen had left and he'd shut up shop for the night and gone upstairs to his room he found the albino stretched in one of his chairs, regarding him blankly from beneath the brim of his felt hat.

'You told me you didn't need an assistant. You told me you weren't giving anybody a job,' the albino said accusingly.

'How did you get in here?'

'You of all people should see that you could have done

me a good turn. You're a Jew. You must know what it's like to be out there on your own. Like me.'

'How did you get in here?' Meyerson repeated stupidly.

'Came up the stairs while you were down in the shop. It was easy. If you'd employed me as a security guard, then this wouldn't have happened.'

'Get out or I'll call the police,' said Meyerson.

Gus walked over to the door. 'I'm going. I wouldn't stay where I wasn't wanted.' He made a last attempt. 'You could help me. People like us should stick together. You've got kind eyes. Don't act like a boss.'

'If you're going, go. What are you waiting for?'

'You've locked up downstairs, haven't you? You'll have to let me out. Now, if I worked here I could do that for you.'

Meyerson led the way downstairs and opened the door of the shop and pointed into the darkness.

The albino strode past him. 'That's right. Harden your heart. Throw me out into the night.' The black glasses in their green circles flashed angrily at him.

The albino continued to hang about with the natives who clustered on the pavement in front of the shop, occasionally joining in a game of soccer using an old, bald tennis ball. Meyerson ignored him – so long as he didn't come inside, he told himself, he didn't care what the albino did. But then one day he was in the dispensary checking his drugs cupboard when he heard Maureen scream. Hurrying into the shop he saw her up the ladder, restocking the gift-wrapped bath salts that were specially packed in cut-glass bowls and which he kept for safety on a high shelf. Gus was at the window, his nose pressed up against it, his breath misting the glass through which Meyerson could see the green circles of his lenses. The albino's nose was white, so hard was it pushed up against the glass, and he was staring straight at Maureen's legs. He hurried Maureen into the back of the shop and calmed her down. When he came out Gus was gone. The chemist's heart seethed with anger against the albino.

'It's just that I've never seen one of them, not a real one,

Mr Meyerson. I know they've got pink eyes and funny hair, but I didn't even know what this was, staring at me through the window. There was this face with those funny green rings round its eyes and the nose all squashed up against the window. I feel a real fool now that I know what it is. Shame, poor thing. Imagine what it must be like to be an albino. I mean it's bad enough to be black, but to be – nothing!'

'Don't you waste your sympathy on him. He's got enough cheek to take care of himself.'

'Yes, I know. But just imagine,' Maureen persisted.

He thought no more about the albino until his friend Michaelis delivered the special new line in bronzing agents. He was telling her how the roll-on applicator worked, or if you preferred, how the spray ran a yellow-brown stripe down your forearm. 'It's all the rage, I believe. Except this way you get your tan in the comfort of your own home. You don't have to go to Durban. That's the beauty of it.' Maureen took the can and idly sprayed the back of her hand with it.

'I was hoping you'd see it that way,' Meyerson said, gazing fondly at her plump forearms. 'You'll do it for me, won't you?'

'I wasn't thinking of that. What this needs to show it off at its best is somebody really – white. I was thinking of the albino.'

Instinctively Meyerson recoiled from the idea. It would mean going back to Gus. It would mean asking him into the shop. It would mean, in effect, giving him a job, going back on everything he had said.

'It's putting him to some good use, Mr Meyerson.'

He looked into the girl's shining eyes and gave way. Not only did he give way, but he astonished himself by going on to praise her brilliant thinking. It was a wonderful idea, it would pull the people in, it would be something they'd never seen before, he really had to hand it to her; in fact, he said, with downcast eyes and a shy smile, he really had been neglecting her, she was far too good and too clever to spend her time replacing stock. Why, he really should make her – his partner. Through lowered lashes he watched to see what effect this had on her and felt her astonished blush to be a great victory.

'Yes,' he said kindly. 'It's putting him to some use.'

The albino's reaction to the offer was not particularly gracious. He haggled over a fee and annoyed Meyerson by insisting on being paid according to the value of what he called his 'time', when it was perfectly apparent that he had more time on his hands than he knew what to do with. And then he insisted on being taken to the shop and shown the products before giving his final consent. Maureen arranged a table in the front window with a white cloth over it on which the range of bronzing agents stood. Gus faced them across the table with his arms folded protectively across his chest, his hat pulled down low over his ridiculous sunglasses. Meyerson demonstrated on Maureen, who was smiling reassuringly at the albino, what he wanted done. The roll-on was to be used on the right forearm and the spray on the left. He didn't intend to cover more than a few square inches, and in this way he calculated that there would be enough skin area on Gus's arms, above and below, to last him for at least three demonstrations.

'Nowhere else,' said the albino slowly, 'I won't be tanned nowhere else. Except only on my hands and arms. Right?'

'Don't you worry about a thing,' Maureen assured him. 'You're in good hands here. We'll look after you.'

'Thanks, Missus. As the only real white man, I need it,' the albino said gratefully.

On the morning of the demonstration Gus arrived promptly and stood before the table rather nervously. Maureen persuaded him to take off his hat. He did so very reluctantly, explaining that to him the sunshine was extremely dangerous. He was one of those who could suffer positive harm by getting a tan. And that meant protecting the top of his head. His scalp, he told her, was tremendously sensitive to sunlight. Maureen sympathised. He had lovely hair, it was like milk.

'It's very thin hair,' said the albino.

'But beautiful. You really ought to show it off.' She took

off his jacket and hung it up and then helped him to roll up his sleeves. Around mid-morning with the shop half full of curious onlookers the demonstration of how to give yourself a tan in your own home got under way.

As Maureen had predicted, it was a great success. People came to see the albino as much as to see the product. As Maureen explained to him, Gus was something new and every product needed a gimmick and he was a very rare gimmick, there was nothing really like him, she said. She compared him, after a lot of thought, to a kind of unicorn. Meyerson was thrilled at the success of the scheme, even if he felt that Maureen might have been a little less considerate in her dealings with the albino. She said they had to make allowances. He warned her to be careful, that Gus would only misinterpret her kindness for weakness and exploit her sympathy and her kind woman's heart. He complained about Gus's sunglasses, pointing out to her that it made several small children in the front row very frightened to see the strange man staring blankly back at them and the cheap green frames didn't help either. He counted it as a small success when Maureen agreed with him.

The next day when the albino turned up for the demonstration, Meyerson saw that he was wearing a new pair of sunglasses – a very elegant pair with thin gold frames – and he appeared to have swopped his old felt hat, for he wore in its place a crisp white panama with a red ribbon. On that second morning it was difficult to move in the shop, and when Maureen had rolled the golden colouring onto the albino's right arm and sprayed his left there was ragged applause from the audience, and afterwards Meyerson sold out nearly all his stock.

On the third and last morning the albino arrived attended by a band of Africans who stayed outside and peered through the window. Twice Meyerson chased them away; they only regrouped and returned the moment he re-entered the shop, which was full by mid-morning, and among the audience he noticed Mrs Boersma. Gus entered nonchalantly, tossed his panama onto the counter and allowed

Maureen to take his jacket; it was still, Meyerson noticed with some satisfaction, the ugly sports coat he'd first seen him in. Then Gus slumped in the chair and held out an arm in a very languid fashion and in the way Meyerson had seen rich women doing in photographs when they went to their manicurists. His anger against the albino mounted. They were all the same. Give them an inch. Meyerson took up a position near the front door where he could both see the proceedings and keep an eye on the excited band of Africans peering through the window. The albino was being quite insufferable. He was quite literally basking in the attention he was being given and in Maureen's solicitous arrangements for his comfort. Meyerson supposed that he couldn't ever in his life have enjoyed this lavish attention. He had a scowling, urgent look about him, an intensity that you caught some sign of in the leaping muscle in his jaw and neck when he rubbed his chin reflectively. Then there was the extraordinary milk-white hair. He'd had a go at persuading Maureen to remove his dark glasses altogether. But she went into the sensitivity of his eyes and the dangers of sunlight and even harsh artificial light and pleaded against it.

'You know, Mr Meyerson, they're really quite pink. Can you believe it?'

Meyerson was aghast at this news. It wasn't the pinkness, he didn't care what colour the albino's eyes were. But he hated the idea that Maureen had seen them.

They ran into their first snag at the demonstration when Maureen discovered there wasn't much flesh left on the arms for her to roll or spray, and even though Gus, with a great show of patience, allowed Maureen to roll his shirt sleeves up to the top of his arms, the audience weren't particularly satisfied. Mrs Boersma spoke for them.

'That's a tanning applicator you've got there, isn't it? Why don't you paint it on his body? Hands and arms are all very well but we get tanned on those when we do our gardening.'

Meyerson acted quickly, striding across the room. 'Will you take off your shirt?' he whispered in the albino's ear.

'I won't. It's not part of the deal, Meyerson. You paid for my arms. My arms you get.'

'It won't hurt, I promise. I'll do it very carefully.' Maureen reached over and squeezed the albino's hand comfortingly.

'I'm up against it,' Meyerson hissed. 'Can't you see they expect something? If you disappoint my audience, you sabotage my sales. Now take off that damned shirt and let Maureen here put the spray on you. Or you can get out of here right now and forget about any money.'

'Certainly not.'

'I'll only do a very little bit,' Maureen told the albino; 'around the shoulders should be enough, the top of the arms, it needn't be more than that. Please. For me.'

The albino reached up and undid the first button.

'For God's sake, get a move on,' Meyerson whispered.

'You think you can do what you like, Meyerson. You think because you're the boss you've got me just where you want me. You think you own this part of Africa so you can do anything.'

Meyerson nodded. 'Yes.' And he felt a bruising, surging joy of that affirmation. 'Yes, I can.'

Gently Maureen drew off the albino's shirt.

The audience clapped and cheered at the icy white, faintly speckled and distantly pink body now emerging into the fluorescent light. Meyerson noticed that Maureen's lips were trembling.

'Give him a spray,' Meyerson ordered.

Maureen raised the can and sprayed a little of the tanning lotion between Gus's shoulder blades.

He writhed. 'It's damn cold!'

'Stand still, dammit!' Meyerson snapped. 'Give him some more.'

Maureen sprayed a straight line down his spine. Her hand was shaking. Gus bellowed again.

'Ladies and gentlemen, see what a lovely gold effect you get,' the chemist rejoiced.

'Turn him round now,' somebody yelled.

'Yes, do him in the front!' Mrs Boersma shrilled.

But the albino had had enough. He was reaching for his shirt. Maureen stood in front of him, not knowing what to say. The calls for more grew louder. Some in the audience began to stamp their feet. They thought they were being cheated. An atmosphere of mockery was growing and with it grew Meyerson's fury. The albino presented his naked back to the audience; they saw it crossed with golden weals of the spray and he was beginning to pull his shirt back down over his head. Meyerson snatched it away from him and taking the man in a fierce, burly hug he lifted him off his feet, turned him with his chest to the audience and mouthed frantically at the bewildered and astonished Maureen.

'Do him in front.' He could see the agony in her eyes and he repeated his order. The girl stared at him and at Gus, who was struggling frantically, emitting high-pitched little squeals as he tried desperately to break free from the chemist's hug.

'Why doesn't he take off his glasses? We want to see his eyes!' The suggestion was strongly put by somebody in the audience.

Gus's struggles increased in violence.

'For God's sake hurry up, woman,' Meyerson implored.

Duty overcame her softer feelings and Maureen lifted the can, steadying it with both hands in the manner of someone taking very careful aim at a target with a revolver. But in spite of her careful alignment of the nozzle the jet she emitted never reached its target. Or pehaps its target, by now grown wild and frantic, managed somehow to shift his captor, for the spray hit the chemist in the eyes and the blinding pain drove him off the albino and down onto the floor.

It was at this point, he heard later, that the crowd turned really ugly and Gus fled for the door which had been opened by his entranced and amazed black friends who had watched the entire proceedings through the plate glass, and Gus, naked to the waist, bare-headed, ran down the street in the sunshine which was so bad for his skin, and that Maureen

Gwass, his Maureen, ran after him until at the end of the street, it was said, she stopped and she took off her white chemist's coat, covered his head and shoulders with it and after that they disappeared.

All this they told him, because of course he saw nothing; it was some hours before his eyes, properly treated, dressed and rested, allowed him to see anything at all, and even then for days afterwards, because of some agent in the spray, they were apt, disconcertingly and without warning, to weep great tears.

The incident made Meyerson's name, there was no doubt of that; if before he'd been on the up and up, now he'd achieved the status of a celebrity. Everyone knew him. His turnover doubled. Of Maureen and Gus nothing was heard. They seemed to have disappeared off the face of the earth.

It was his friend Michaelis who one day brought news unexpectedly, when they were dining at the Railway Hotel. He'd actually seen them in a casino, in a neighbouring African state where he had been spending the weekend. He knew Maureen, of course, and he said he recognized her as soon as he saw her, sitting behind the reception desk, where the hostesses who danced with the farmers waited for the customers. She wore an electric-blue dress, he said, with a great white rose at her breast. And Gus, well, he'd seen him when he went to play the tables. Gus was a croupier, his hair now puffed, pomaded, the pale, gleaming pride of the man showed clearly, a bouffant hair-do, Michaelis called it, and of course the fancy dark glasses; he was the preening white peacock of the gaming tables.

'A gimmick, you see. An albino croupier.' There was no missing the note of grudging admiration. 'I know a gimmick when I see one.'

'Maureen too,' said Meyerson. And he thought to himself, but what life can they have? He saw Maureen, probably blowsy now, in her evening dress and her white rose, and Gus, glossily conceited at his success, the terrible pink skin and the dark glasses, raking chips across the tables. He spoke aloud: 'A gimmick, OK, but this is something more. I mean it's going native, isn't it?'

Michaelis looked surprised. 'Well, I don't think you could call it that, see what I mean? It's not here, you see, it's *there* that they've set up. Still basically bush country, really. Where they are you can do what you like. I mean it's anyone's country there. Nobody gives a damn. You get my drift? You can do what you like with whoever you like. They think they're getting civilized, what with their independence and their casino. But it's frontier. Raw, bloody frontier.'

Meyerson presided in his shop in the suburb which had a quiet, settled, established look to it. It was almost what you might have called trim. Houses there were sought after because it was convenient for the city centre. He became famous in the suburbs after the albino business. He prospered. And every penny he made was a knife in his heart.

My Stigmata

I remember the morning I found that I had the wounds. I got up and went downstairs to the bathroom, holding my side, the pain was that bad. On my way I met my landlady, Doris Clench. 'I think I've got the stigmata, Mrs Clench,' I said.

'Garn,' she said.

'No, really.' Nodding vigorously, I pushed past her to the bathroom, the better to examine the extent of the damage.

My left side was pierced by a red raw wound about the size of a shilling. My hands and feet carried the traditional marks. They looked like bullet holes, dead centre through each palm and neat, with no ragged edges, covered by a transparent membrane through which the red flesh gleamed. Anxiously I explored my hairline in the mirror for signs of the crown of thorns, but it seemed that I was spared that at least. On second thoughts, it didn't cheer me up much because I remembered that exterior stigmatisation may be preceded by invisible stigmata, as happened with the celebrated Padre Pio. But then Pio had been a natural candidate for the honour, and honour it is among mystics. What with his levitation during the consecration of the mass and his almost supernatural percipience in the confessional, you could have said that he was asking for it. But not me. It was only because I was a lapsed Catholic that I had recognized the symptoms, but for the rest I was barely a Christian, and I certainly wasn't religious. Something was very wrong, somewhere.

As I made my careful way up the stairs to my room, I met my neighbour, Mr Patel. We did not get on too well. He had a succession of icy blondes coming to his room most nights and the bumps and groans and shrieks in the small hours kept me awake. I hadn't had a decent night's sleep in weeks. Mr Patel made the point of apologizing to me on every possible occasion for the exuberance of his lovers. They became too excited, he explained. I did not want to speak to him, but one look at his face showed me that there was no escaping. His smooth hand rested on my sleeve. 'Courage, my friend.'

'I suppose Mrs Clench told you?'

He nodded and patted me on the shoulder gingerly. He kept glancing at my hands which were sunk in the pockets of my dressing gown.

'It is a holy affliction.'

'It's a bloody tragedy.' As I fumbled at the door of my room with my key, I noticed that he had not moved and was gazing up the stairwell at me, his eyes liquid with concern.

'The love of God can hurt a man,' he called.

I managed to get my door open. 'Yes,' I said, 'especially when he gets too excited.'

I went into my room and sat on my bed for what must have been at least an hour, maybe more. It was some while later, anyway, that I snapped out of it. There was no point sitting there like a dummy. I had to get out and about. I put on gloves and carpet slippers and went downstairs.

Outside the sun was shining and the sky was a blank and lovely blue. The sun lit up the vacant little park across the way, the 'gardens' from which the neighbourhood took its name, with its locked gates to which only the oldest in the Victorian boarding houses flanking the road had keys and there were fewer of those each year.

Obviously there was no question of my going to work, wearing gloves and carpet slippers, my body a dull ache. I could not go back to my desk at the Imperial Insurance Company and continue writing all risks policies covering the jewels of rich women. I could not give up my mind to anything at that moment but to the control of the pain that bent me double, dogged my footsteps and held my hands tightly.

There was nothing for it but to see the doctor. I sat in the waiting room, leaning up against the frosted glass, reading an article in *Life* about outer space and the universe and how if one imagined the sun as an orange then the earth was no bigger than a pea, or something, a hundred miles away. At last the light went on above one of the brown-painted doors and the nurse called my name and showed me in to the doctor.

He was very kind. I removed my left glove and he made a thorough examination of the wound. 'A nasty business,' he said.

'I have another on my right hand,' I told him.

'Gracious me!' he snorted, 'you've really been in the wars, haven't you? We'd better have your shirt off.'

'Actually, I have two identical holes in my feet,' I said, as casually as I could, struggling with my shirt buttons. I took off all my clothes then and lay down on the bed.

He drew in his breath sharply when he saw me. 'Who has injured you like this?' he demanded.

'I think it was an accident,' I said.

'Well,' he said, after examining me closely, 'the least I can do is to dress them. Though, I'll hand it to you, you've kept them remarkably clean without the use of bandages and antiseptic. How you managed it, I don't know. Anyway, I'll give you something for them and then, remember please, a clean dressing every morning.' He bent to examine the wounds again. They fascinated him, I could see that. Clearly, he didn't want me to put on my clothes yet. 'Remarkable symmetry about them,' he said. 'Of course, if you had come to me earlier, I'd have stitched them for you. It's too late now. They're healing.'

I walked home. Mrs Clench and her daughters awaited me in the hallway. Mrs Clench's daughters attended a convent school. All looked at me with earnest eyes.

'So we're off to work, are we?' Mrs Clench asked, not unkindly.

Her daughters eyed me hopefully. What did they expect me to do? I smiled as best I could and went upstairs to my room. The pain was no worse. No better, but no worse. The dressings the doctor had used were comfortable and maybe he was right about the wounds healing. Voices were raised in the hallway below. I lay down on my bed and closed my eyes. Clearly, the news was getting around.

In the morning I dressed the wounds. I could detect no change in their glassy surface although they seemed to throb less painfully. I put on my gloves and carpet slippers and went down for a walk. A small crowd had gathered outside the door. Mrs Clench was addressing interested neighbours. They stopped talking when they saw me and looked embarrassed. Two mild men in grey raincoats pressed forward.

'Hansome, of *The Times*,' said the taller of the two, holding out his hand.

'How do you do.' I kept my hands firmly in my pockets.

'My photographer, Pounder, Rutland Pounder.' His companion nodded cheerily. 'I wonder if you would mind if we spoke to you briefly about the rather strange situation in which you find yourself?'

The neighbours smiled encouragingly. They knew, their smiles assured me, that perhaps this wasn't a proper occasion for the press, but it was after all *The Times*.

'Come inside,' I said, 'we can talk in my room.'

The pictures the next morning were very good and the story beside them was concise and lucid, not at all sensational. I found myself reading it with interest. Although now a stigmatic, I was very far from being an expert on the subject. I wondered if the doctor who had treated me took *The Times*.

As I neared home with the newspaper I saw the neighbours gathered in what was now a regular knot on the steps before Mrs Clench's front door. I saw, too, a bus parked by the kerb, a school bus. Ranged next to it was a long, orderly, crocodile of convent girls. I recognized the uniform as being the same as that worn by the young Clench girls. I stopped dead and then, of course, just as I realised I should get away quickly, they saw me. A fat, brisk nun with silver hair and rosy cheeks trotted up to me and bobbed a knee. She and her girls were there, she explained frankly, in the hopes of meeting me. The young Clench girls had talked at school about their mother's lodger who had been blessed with Christ's five glorious wounds. Nobody had paid very much attention to them until the report appeared in *The Times*. She and her girls had not come to stare, but to look and to marvel at the works of God.

'It's a very wonder the marks the good Jesus puts upon a man.' Her Irish lisp conveyed her sentiment and I was reminded of my schooldays, when it was always an Irish voice that led the general prayers in the parish church after confessions each Friday. Mind you, it was a Jewish boy who'd led the prayers in the classroom when the bell rang on the hour and the class rose to recite the Hail Mary as they did again at twelve o'clock for the Angelus. From then on all prayers for me were prayed in Irish or Jewish voices and even the tones of those voices in banal conversation took on a sacral quality recalling the giant Christ who swung in agony upon his cross above the high altar in the cool gloom of the parish church when we prayed our communal prayers on those Friday mornings after confession. Outside one could hear the doves calling in the fir trees. It was very peaceful and miles from school and almost worth praying for. Often I was tempted to sneak out of the side door as we left the church to straggle back to the classroom and to hide myself behind the hedge that flanked the garden and orchards and sit there in the sun. Just sit there, quietly, untouched by anything but my own thoughts as the sun moved higher in the sky, warming my bones.

'I'm sorry,' I said, looking into her blue eyes, 'but what can I say? I have all the wounds, but this is not the place . . .'

'Except the crown,' she said.

'Except the crown,' I agreed. 'I've been spared that.'

'It takes some differently, my dear,' she said. 'Now, Maria Razzi of Chio, why, she had the thorny crown alone.'

'You've made a study of it, Sister?'

She beamed. 'We're doing a project in class.'

She took her girls away, with some giggling and downcast looks in the rear files of the crocodile. She seemed moved. I walked inside without a glance at the little groups of people who stood on either side of the street before the rows of silent houses, talking and staring.

That tour of the convent girls and their sweet-cheeked teacher was the start of a wave of publicity that hit that afternoon and continued for a week. In that time I was assailed by people wherever I went, wanting to know how I felt, the extent of my pain, the shape of my wounds, the health of my soul, the heat of my faith, my plans for the future. Worst were those who made joking allusions to Doubting Thomas and licked their lips, not daring to ask me out loud to let them see and touch my stigmata.

The day after the visit of the convent girls, a great scarlet coachload of bishops drew up outside Mrs Clench's house, and a deputation of their lordships entered to greet me. They had come, I was assured, not to gape, but to congratulate me. They had learnt that I was an unwilling stigmatic and so they hoped that I would not take it amiss and feel even more put upon were they to offer me their warmest greetings and prayerful good wishes. They were immensely grateful for this wonder that had been worked in me, and however vicarious their satisfaction might appear to me to be, I was respectfully asked to bear with them in their joy at the greatest fillip Christianity had received in England for decades. Stigmata had become more common in comparatively recent times, perhaps through devotion to the Sacred Heart, but that was hardly an English practice. Indeed my stigmata seemed to fill the bishops with much the same confidence and enthusiasm as my role at the Imperial Insurance Company did for rich women by making certain that their jewels, even if by some horrid catastrophe reduced to their natural elements, would retain their value in our books at least.

I saw the bishops off, talking happily, all smiles and waves, and turned inside. I was moving a little more easily. The pain was still there. But it was no worse. It seemed hard now to imagine a time when I had not had this dull ache in hands, feet and side. Perhaps I was getting used to it.

Mr Patel stood in the entrance hall holding the public telephone which served us all in the house.

'It's the *Psychic News* on the line,' he whispered, covering the mouthpiece. 'They want to talk to you.'

I looked at him. I could think of nothing to say.

'I shall tell them that you are indisposed.'

I went upstairs to bed. I washed my wounds and applied the antiseptic and dressings the doctor had given me but I did so more out of habit than conviction. The wounds seemed unaffected by the treatment. They seemed to have a being of their own, affixed to myself, but independent of me. Then I settled into a long, dreamless sleep.

In the morning I awoke almost refreshed and reflected that, perhaps, my strangeness was being made too much of, by myself as well as by others. Men had fragile, paper-thin skins, which wrinkled and tore easily. My tears were coincidentally localised, that was all. Altogether, I decided, there was too much fuss being made. My stigmata had become too much of a good thing.

It was early yet and the house was asleep. I decided to take a walk, donned my carpet slippers and gloves, and went quietly downstairs. But I had no sooner opened the door and taken a breath of the morning freshness when windows and doors opened all around me. There were faces at panes. Dogs barked, the milkman arrived and housewives appeared on the doorsteps with their dogs and children and husbands and gazed at me. I lost my nerve and closed the door. Perhaps I would venture out later.

Mrs Clench faced me in the dark hallway. She smiled encouragingly. In her hands she held a copy of *The Times*. I took it. She had opened it at the centre page which carried the editorials. Her eyes were shining. I followed her trembling finger and understood the cause of her excitement: I was the subject of the third editorial.

*What can be said of this young man? He has been
visited by a strange and novel experience. One which
is perhaps even more shocking since it comes to him
without either his knowledge or his encouragement.
His behaviour in this matter has been exemplary. So
much more so than that of those people who have
taken an interest in his religious experience. We salute
him. It might be thought by some in these Islands that
the phenomenon which he has experienced is confined
to those who embrace the Church of Rome. This
extraordinary, some will say miraculous, event, has
given proof, if proof were needed, that the division of
faith is the failure of our times – and nonsense, to boot.
Besides, there is no room, surely, as recent and bloody
events not far removed from us have shown, for this
sort of sectarian prejudice.*

'Well . . . yes,' I thought.

Sometime later I slipped outside by the back door. I could not stand being cooped up any longer. I put on my gloves and slippers and, after a moment's thought, a black woollen balaclava helmet. No one recognized me as I walked swiftly through the morning sunshine. I came to a pond, spanned by a narrow little bridge, where people stopped and gathered to talk.

'They say that he has holes, gaping holes, nail marks in his hands and feet, Doris says, though she's never seen them,' a little old lady, well wrapped in green coat and muffler, was saying to another in a red trench coat and wellingtons.

'Ever so painful they must be, too,' the other agreed. 'I saw the pictures in *The Times*. And him not even the least bit religious.'

'I know,' said the little lady, 'it's not nice, is it?'

'Of course you can't believe everything you read in the papers, now can you? I mean, Doris didn't actually *see* these wounds, did she? I mean, she saw the photos in *The Times*, same as we did. That's all. And she says that he doesn't go to work any longer.'

'You've got a point there,' her friend nodded.

'And you know, sometimes I think these people bring these things on themselves. Besides, we all have our problems, don't we?'

But she had lost the attention of her companion who had turned and was looking straight at me.

'Didn't you say that he dressed in gloves and carpet slippers?'

'So Doris said.'

Then they were both looking at me. I put my head down and walked away entering my boarding house by the back door. I had hoped to avoid meeting anybody. But once again Mrs Clench accosted me at the foot of the stairs. I eyed her defiantly through my balaclava helmet. In the silence I became aware of my heavy breathing.

She eyed me with faint curiosity. 'No change?'

I shook my head and went up to my room, undressed and got into bed. By seven o'clock that evening, I was still awake. Several bumps, a groan and a giggle behind the wall told me that Mr Patel's lovers were once again becoming too excited.

The Kugel

Joel Wolferman came up to university in a powder-blue Porsche, smiled often, spent money, and left suddenly and the manner of his leaving so grievously wounded the student body that the scar is still visible. His time on the campus, when people looked back at it, came to seem a watershed; they talked of life 'before Wolferman' in the way their parents talked of 'before the war'. You could say that the manifestation of Wolferman in university life became, in student terms, the equivalent of the serpent's appearance in Eden. He marked the Fall. After Wolferman an age of innocence was no more; after Wolferman, Eddie Springer, one-time big student leader who had not taken an exam in five years and was definitely the old man of the campus, politically aware, often arrested and widely admired, began to take annual examinations with conventional regularity, to pass them and to become, as everyone knows, an authority on comparative African government with a famous thesis on 'Ethnicity in the Gold Mines', which was later published.

After Wolferman, the kugels (deceptively named for the sleek missiles they were, from those sweet heavy puddings stuffed with raisins) redoubled their social energies, flashing hungrily across town in their Italian sports cars, stood strategically poised on the library steps sunning their breasts and reactivated the marriage market with a vengeance, hunted down medics, dentists and lawyers-to-be without quarter, and cursed all politicians.

Wolferman got off to an awkward start because he became so quickly and in so many senses notable. Tall and dark with a mass of black curls and a pointed chin, with eyes of some indeterminate colour, blue mixing with green, 'salted candle-flame eyes', as Judith Klein, one of his disappointed hunters once described them; the new freshman was apparently an orphan yet the fellow clearly viewed himself as being already adult and this daring maturity, this air of authority in a young man who should by rights be all fingers and thumbs, intrigued, infuriated or attracted all who came to know him.

His uncle had sent him up from some remote country town; Ted Malkin found out that Wolferman's uncle had made his fortune by importing cheap labour from the neighbouring states in the north for the gold mines. He'd been a broker in human muscle, as Malkin put it. Wolferman had told him about the beastly trade without the hint of a blush and seemed (Malkin again) to think bloody well nothing of it. Wolferman moved into Malkin's building where students occupied the warren of small rooms on the eight floors; only Wolferman didn't simply take a room, he took the penthouse unused for years and built for the exclusive enjoyment of the entrepreneur who had put up the block, a great place designed for a man with money. Enormous picture windows looking out across the city to the distant flat-topped mine dumps, pale, gleaming yellow in the evening sun, their sides roughened with stubborn climbing grass. Into this place Joel Wolferman moved with great panoply. Ted Malkin in his little bedsitter on the third floor watched it all, saw the huge pantechnicon arrive and the sweating removal men bossed by an Indian with gold teeth carry the new man's things upstairs.

'He arrived with this big van and out of it came more furniture than you need to open a department store, up the stairs he goes at the head of a band of sweating lackeys and proceeds to allow himself to be installed up there on the roof of the world like some great, bloody pasha. Can you believe it? Can you imagine how much that penthouse cost?

I met him later, knocking on all the doors and inviting everyone up for a drink. There must have been about a dozen of us, we sat on packing cases and drank whisky. Whisky! We stared at his furniture which is tubular with leather and stared at the view. You could see right across the city towards the gold mines – like bloody executives! He's got these spidery pictures, Eddie, porno pictures, at least that's what they look like to me, drawings, you know, men, women. Everything bloody curling and dangling. He tells me they're going up on the walls. Imagine that; he sat there in this amazing white suit and white shoes, sipping whisky and telling us he intended to hang up these porno pictures on the walls. Bought with the fortune made from selling black man's sweat. And, *no*, it doesn't worry him. Why should it? All this without a blush. What with his weird clothes and all, and his frightfully gung-ho manner, and his views of the gold mines, this guy is too much. You wait until you meet him, Eddie.'

Sturdy, energetic, cheerfully uncouth, stubby-fingered, Eddie Springer with his sharp intelligent face and his lank yellow hair was at the height of his fame on the campus. He'd just been inside, in solitary confinement, and this for the second time, for a full forty-three days and only got out because of the intervention of some smart lawyer his parents had hired in the face of Eddie's protestations. The story was already all over the campus about how he'd been picked up outside the prison gates by his old folks who were just about to drive away when these two security policemen came running out with a big red biscuit tin and in the biscuit tin were all the odds and ends he'd left behind in his cell, his tooth-brush, his comb, and his handkerchiefs and these were handed over to them with many salaams and fixed smiles and Eddie's parents had actually gone and thanked the cops feeling tremendously impressed at their kindness. Everyone heard about how Eddie gave them hell for that, saying that they shouldn't have accepted the biscuit tin and certainly should never have said 'thank you' to a couple of gorillas, as if they approved of them, paid thugs who'd stood him in a corner for eighteen hours without sleep and threatened to ram a broom handle up his arse and generally given him a hard time. Eddie's parents, the legend went, had snapped right back that that sort of talk was all very well but they didn't really suppose the police enjoyed having to do what they had to do any more than Eddie himself did, but there was after all such a thing as elementary courtesy. That phrase became a catch-word among the radical students for a few weeks, and it appeared on a banner in the very next demonstration: 'Elementary courtesy for political prisoners'. All who saw it agreed that it was absolutely rich.

And so it was that when Joel Wolferman came to classes for the first time, Eddie Springer who was strolling in the sunshine with Barney Tembisa, the black medical student, crossed over the road in Samaritan fashion and spoke to Wolferman with a naturalness which was one of his most admired qualities, and even more admirable in this case since Wolferman was wearing a dark blue pin-striped suit, patent leather shoes like gleaming black pools beneath his turn-ups, and a rich red rose in his buttonhole. Passers-by stopped to witness this odd confrontation, the intensely serious Springer in his sandals and old brown corduroys and the strange new man in his amazingly unsuitable suit.

'Wolferman? My name is Springer, students' council, and since you're a new guy here I was wondering how you felt about the issues.'

The new man gave a genial smile. 'What issues?'

Eddie Springer drew Barney forward. 'I have one right here. Barney Tembisa, medical student, third year. A living issue. If the government has its way it will kick Barney off the campus and people like him who aren't white will be packed off to some bush college in the back of beyond, if they're lucky. We're fighting for people like Barney, to keep this university open for people of all races. We're fighting for academic freedom.'

Wolferman reached out and shook Tembisa's hand. 'It must be hard to be a living issue,' he said, carefully polite.

Barney Tembisa was clearly taken aback. Tembisa's looks

gave a misleading impression of the man. His rather sad brown eyes and his plump, round, kindly face in which a pair of prominent cheekbones were the only things to interrupt an almost perfect circularity deceived people when they contemplated his white coat and carefully pressed grey flannels; on the one hand he was clearly going to make a fine doctor one day, on the other he was all too likely to end up in jail before he qualified as he made no secret of his ambition to see a total end to the colour bar and the destruction of the government and all its works.

'I'm not an issue in myself,' Barney said.

'He's too modest. If he isn't – who is?' Springer demanded. 'We're fighting a war and you can either join us or you can while away your time on the sports fields and eventually be caught by the kugels. The kugels, in case you don't know, are those rich girls with names like Lorraine, and Wanda and Michelle, usually driving Alfa Romeos, whose brothers are clerks on the Stock Exchange or studying to be dentists and whose fathers are rich business men in the shady suburbs; they don't come to university to take a degree, they're here to become known, to look around and have fun and find a husband. A kugel is a sweet, clinging kind've kid, who comes on round and soft like a sugary cake, but is really a kind of hunter killer. You get lots of them here. Usually they have big breasts. It's either them or the issues, Wolferman.'

'And if I don't like the choice?'

'Life is choosing, Wolferman. Have a word with Barney. He'll explain.' And with a burning look, he went on his way.

'Eddie had this thing about big breasts,' Tembisa said, smiling. 'He's prejudiced against them. Maybe because his girl-friend, Belinda, was a kugel with breasts once. But then she saw the light. She was politicised. She runs a crêche for the children of the black cleaners here. As a result, her breasts have disappeared, as it were. They say she wears vests now. Medically speaking that's not possible, but politics can work miracles.' The black man was faintly amused.

'Seriously, Eddie wants to know if you'll run with the kugels or come and join us in the fight against oppression.'

'And you are one of the oppressed?' Wolferman was clearly sympathetic.

Barney nodded slowly. 'I suppose I am.'

Thoughtfully Wolferman sniffed the rose in his lapel. 'I'm definitely against oppression.'

'Well then what do you say?'

Wolferman gave his charming smile. 'Would you like to come to a party?'

Eddie Springer never went to that party. He never went to any of Joel's parties and there were many of them. Barney Tembisa went but then as Eddie said gloomily, he supposed that Barney could afford it, being who he was and coming from where he did. He deserved to go to parties. Lots of other people went to the parties in the big penthouse. The porno pictures on the walls turned out to be drawings by Aubrey Beardsley; the identification immediately made by the fine arts students greatly disappointed Eddie Springer. People fell silent in Wolferman's enormous apartment, gazed at the thick white wall-to-wall carpet, the massive hi-fi, the steel and leather chairs and whispered about the huge four-poster bed, shook their heads over the money it must have cost, and drank his liquor with an enthusiasm which could never quite disguise their sense of disbelief that anyone could really live on this level. Joel Wolferman introduced the students to a taste for enjoyment which dulled political commitment by encouraging a mood of sticky camaraderie. Eddie wondered aloud whether Wolferman was not perhaps a government agent placed on the campus to confuse the issues and weaken opposition. Belinda, Eddie's girlfriend, talked of him as that overdressed, shining fool. Ted Malkin ran his hand through his thick blond hair and blew harshly between his teeth when he mentioned his name, a usual sign of irritability, lamenting the fact that Wolferman lived in the same building.

'I'm just getting in from some demonstration, tired and thirsty and maybe I've been kicked around a bit and I'm walking up the stairs and who comes down, dressed for tennis but not just for bloody tennis, but dressed to the nines as if he was going off to bloody Wimbledon or somewhere, but Wolferman, swinging his racquet with that tally-ho look of his and wanting to know when I'm going to give him a game. It pisses me off, I can tell you, it damn well pisses me off.'

Eddie Springer's mood grew blacker. Damn good people were getting drunk on Wolferman's booze up in his penthouse. The man was threatening political education on the campus. It was in this mood that Springer confronted Wolferman in the famous 'Who pushed who?' incident. Nobody saw it. All one had was Eddie's account, spoken painfully through bruised lips.

'I said to him quite plainly, I said, your life style spits in the face of decent people, of people like Barney Tembisa. And he answers me, d'you know how he answers me? By asking if I play golf? Did you know he was buying a boat so he can go sailing at the weekends? When he's not playing rugby, or rallying in that ridiculous Porsche. I said to him that playing golf wasn't very much use to a black student living in two rooms in the township and expecting to be kicked out of university tomorrow. All he said to that was that golf was a funny game and you never knew until you tried. I reminded him that his money came from his guardian and his guardian got his money from the sweat of black labour, cheap labour, imported to work on the mines, and he couldn't turn his back on that. But that's exactly what he did, telling me he had to go off and play squash and they never kept the courts if you didn't turn up on time and that's when I put my hand out to stop him, that's all I did, trying to get his attention, and that's when he attacked me.'

At his parties in the penthouse Joel Wolferman told a different story: 'Poor old Eddie became too excited and launched himself at me like a terrier. I plucked him off, gently though, before he did himself any harm and put him down carefully. I'm afraid the trouble is that I just don't seem able to live up to his expectations.' And people continued to climb the eight flights to his place for the music and the great views across the mine dumps and the endless supply of liquor.

There were a few who talked of converting Wolferman's undoubted energy to the cause, like Barney Tembisa, in whom the activity was regarded as a positively saintly thing to do since he had less need than anyone to try and reform Wolferman. Eddie Springer's girlfriend, Belinda, seeing the effect it was having decided that it was about time she spoke her mind and received permission from Eddie to go to his next party, in the course of duty. Ted Malkin in his tiny room on the third floor had done his bit to help. He complained in writing that the loud music interfered with his studies and he succeeded in getting the landlord to impose a midnight limit on the parties and was extremely upset when he was jeered at the very next time he addressed a student meeting.

'You don't care about academic freedom! About people like Barney Tembisa – all you care about are bread and circuses . . .'

'And parties!' came the merciless rejoinder.

The kugels vied with one another to capture Wolferman. Girls like Melissa Dworkin who had been a rag princess, sister to the famous Clara who had gone to live on a kibbutz and had actually shot an Arab during an attack on the settlement, which caused a considerable stir when news came back since Clara had never shown the stamina needed merely to pass first year sociology. He took Melissa out in his Porsche for 'a drive', but it turned out that 'the drive' was actually a rally and she was along to do some rudimentary map-reading. A few months later Melissa was pregnant by an extra-mural articled clerk only in his second year and had to leave; this tragedy was widely ascribed to the disappointment she'd suffered at Wolferman's hands. Then there was Judith Klein, the once slim, pretty Judith with her fondness for skintight yellow leggings and Mexican ponchos who took him shooting on the family's game ranch in Bechuanaland, only to find that Wolferman liked nothing more than to sit up well into the small hours drinking whisky with her father and never seemed to go to bed at all. In the next weeks Judith began eating prodigiously, it was rumoured, and had to be sent to a clinic. Ruthie Shapiro, acknowledged queen of the kugels, got closest to scoring with Wolferman by batting her big brown eyes at him and luring him to her place late at night, slipped away after strategically placing him beside the pool, emerging a few moments later from the changing room quite naked with an invitation to join her in a midnight swim. Wolferman's lightning reaction was to nip across to his car and produce from the boot a costume for each of them, to insist that she put it on, turning his back while she did so and then changing himself while she closed her eyes, then picking her up and repeatedly ducking her in the pool behaving, Ruthie said afterwards, 'like some bloody ten-year-old having a bath with his big sister.' She stopped going to his parties and brooded on her humiliation.

Then Eddie's girlfriend, Belinda, spoke her mind, marching up to Wolferman in her black stretch slacks and her plain white blouse through which could be seen very faintly the straps of the vest she was said to wear, and fixing on him her large blue eyes which bulged just a little but not unattractively, she demanded to know whether Wolferman was deliberately trying to subvert and destroy student opposition to government policies. Wolferman replied that he hoped very much that he had done nothing to injure his fellow students of whom he was tremendously fond. Belinda told him to prove it. Wolferman promptly asked her out to dinner and Belinda was so angry she accepted. He took her to the Mediterranean, the smartest nightclub in town. She sat in the pink plush chair pale with rage and shame and would eat only a little clear soup, a piece of bread, a single piece of ham and she toyed with a glass of wine while she was obliged to watch Wolferman work his way with great expertise through the choicest dishes on the menu. His lobster alone, she computed, cost enough to keep a whole family she knew in the African location in powdered milk for at least a week and then something or other with truffles which followed would have subsidised a soup kitchen. She contained herself in the restaurant but on the way home she'd made him stop the car and threw up on the side of the road. Eddie thought this was a wonderful way of expressing the nausea she must have felt. He called a special meeting of the Students Council.

'The time has come to cut Wolferman out.'

'It will be no good if it's just the politically aware people who stay away from his parties,' Belinda said. 'As long as the kugels keep going they attract all the men.'

'Then we must persuade them to stop,' Eddie said. 'Maybe that won't be too difficult. The kugels are getting just a little pissed off with Mr Joel Wolferman because they reckon he's playing them around. He won't declare himself for them just as he won't declare himself for us. If we combined to freeze him out I reckon we could hurt him. I mean a guy who comes to university has got some obligations, for God's sake. He's got to attend to the way things are. He can't go on doing as he damn well likes.'

'If we can cut him out, it'll really hurt,' Belinda agreed. 'What's clear about Wolferman is that he likes to be liked. You can feel it.'

'Maybe we should give him a last chance,' Barney Tembisa suggested.

Ted Malkin patted the black man's shoulder. 'Barney, you're too damned kind. If anyone is entitled to put the boot into the likes of Wolferman, it's you. Here you are poor and black and coming from the township with nothing and there's Wolferman with his fancy suits and his whisky always living it up and throwing his money about and you can still ask us to give him a chance. It's generous. More, it's damn generous. But it's time for generosity to stop.'

'Did you know that Wolferman is going around saying that racialism doesn't matter to him? He doesn't care about it,' Eddie demanded.

'It's true. He told me in that awful nightclub that he feels nothing about colour,' Belinda confirmed.

Barney smiled ruefully. 'Somehow I don't think that's what he means.'

'Then he should say what he means,' Eddie Springer declared.

Barney shook his head. 'He won't understand why we're doing this.'

The others fell silent in the face of Tembisa's extraordinary tolerance. Belinda gave Barney an agonised look.

'Look Barney,' Springer said gently, 'let's say that we're actually helping him. How else will he understand that he's got to choose where he stands on the issues?'

'But Eddie, don't you see? He doesn't care about issues,' Barney shook his head. 'He's got other, well, feelings. There's love in him, Eddie.'

'Love's for kugels. This is war,' Eddie said. 'He has set himself above us. All of us – kugels as well as radicals and it's in the interest of the whole student body that we take action. Love's all very well but this is a question of principle, as I'm sure Barney would agree. I am going to have a word with Ruthie.'

Here began a period of rare amity on campus, proving, as people said, that when the students felt themselves threatened they would band together, sink the differences between radical and kugel and present a united front. In the meeting between Eddie Springer and Ruthie Shapiro a bargain was struck.

A few days later Wolferman came looking for Eddie Springer on the campus. He was pale and for once, Springer noticed with satisfaction, he wasn't smiling.

'I think I'm the victim of some sort of conspiracy, Springer.'

'Something like this had to happen.'

'What is it exactly that I'm supposed to have done?'

'You haven't understood the way we are. Everything you do, the way you live, deliberately rejects everything we believe in.'

'All I've done is to give a few parties.'

'There's more to life than parties – or golf,' Eddie said, remorselessly sincere.

Wolferman sighed. 'What can I do?'

Eddie sighed a measured sigh he really enjoyed, deep enough for sympathy, long enough to allow him to order his thoughts. 'Well I suppose once upon a time something might have been done, a few protest marches, or a couple of lunch-time demonstrations. Could be that had you even found yourself a kugel it might have helped, but you've gone your own way.'

Wolferman said nothing for a time. He just stood there shaking his head. 'I ask people to my place and no one comes.'

'I warned you, Wolferman.'

'Look Springer, I tell you what, if it will help I'll come on a march.'

Eddie gave an incredulous yelp of laughter. 'I appreciate the offer, but the time for that has passed.'

'Then I'll find myself a kugel,' Wolferman's face was set and serious.

'Sure,' Eddie grinned encouragingly. 'Why don't you try and do that.'

Wolferman seemed prepared to ignore the grinning scepticism with which this encouragement was delivered. 'Okay, I will,' he said.

From that time he was never seen again on the campus. Ted Malkin reported that he'd confined himself to his penthouse. There was something faintly alarming in Wolferman's voice, worrying enough to send Eddie to firm up the alliance with Ruthie who said that she was ninety-nine per cent certain that her girls would hold out against any attempt on the playboy's part to break the boycott. Of course she wasn't saying it could never happen. Her people were only human. But at the moment they were as fixed in their desire to make Wolferman sweat as the radicals were. If he did tempt someone, it would have to be one hell of an offer, Ruthie said, immediate marriage and a Greek honeymoon, at the very least ... Eddie Springer came away grateful for her powerful reassurance.

It was surprising, then, how well Eddie took the news a week or so later than Wolferman had broken the blockade. Ted Malkin overheard someone climbing the stairs to Wolferman's apartment in the early hours of the morning.

The other radicals took it badly. The kugels had betrayed them. It was another Munich, Belinda said and reduced Ruthie Shapiro to tears by heckling her in the canteen with shouts of 'Peace in our time!' and 'Chamberlain!' They were nonplussed when Eddie simply smiled and told them not to worry.

'Don't sweat. We've got the boy boxed in. He can't win now, whatever he does. The big spender with the parties and the view of the gold mines is cut down to size. *Wunderkind* is washed up.'

'You mean that the god has left him,' said Ted Malkin, literary as ever.

'Right. From now on he's just another guy who has been hooked by a kugel.'

'What now?' Belinda demanded.

'That's easy,' said Eddie, 'now we find out who she is. The very next time Ted reports activity in the penthouse we will be ready.'

When the call came Eddie and Belinda moved into Malkin's room. The idea was to keep vigil around the clock; whenever it was that the lovers emerged from their nest the stairs were their only exit and passed Ted's room where the reception committee would be waiting for them.

It seemed as if Wolferman and his kugel had no intention of coming out. Two days and nights passed and no one left the penthouse though several scouting expeditions reported that an ear pressed to the door detected signs of life within. The siege continued.

On the third night, about four in the morning, the secret watchers were shaken by a thunder of boots on the stairs and ran to fling open the door in time to witness a group of uniformed policemen tearing up the stairs, whooping like huntsmen in full cry. One man carried a bright axe in a canvas scabbard. The watchers followed. Other students woken by the noise began emerging from their rooms. Outside the penthouse the policemen paused for a brief council which seemed primarily concerned with deciding who should have the privilege of wielding the bright axe, clearly one of the perks of the job. The council over, and the door breached in moments, the policemen shouldered through the splintered gap followed by the excited students.

Joel Wolferman lay on the big, four-poster dressed in a pair of blue shorts and a white teeshirt advertising a fund to save the white rhino from extinction. He seemed quite unperturbed, almost as if he had been expecting the raid, lying back with a cigarette blowing smoke at the roof. He was, everyone realised once again, a very big fellow and the policemen approached him with caution but Wolferman offered no resistance. Beside him, beneath the heavy white silken bedspread with the Mexican or Aztec pattern woven in gold thread, lay Barney Tembisa. They lay so still they might have been posing for a picture. Indeed, clearly anxious not to miss the opportunity one of the policemen produced a camera and took several shots.

Belinda was never to forget the white bedspread with its gold, geometrical patterns, or, as a policeman with an expert flick tossed it aside, the black man lying on the white sheets utterly naked. Other students were by this time crowding into the bedroom with sleepy cries of bewilderment, trying to peer over the shoulders of those lucky enough to have a view. No one spoke. Tembisa was ordered off the bed and as he got out he shot a look of horrible embarrassment at Belinda and scurried across into a corner crossing his hands before him, his large, soft buttocks shaking. He was handcuffed. Wolferman was handcuffed and continued to lie on the bed, smoking, lifting both hands to his mouth.

Without warning Eddie Springer attacked, throwing himself on Tembisa who tried hopelessly with his manacled hands to push him away but Eddie bore him down, punching and kicking him repeatedly until a policeman pulled him off. Wolferman watched from the bed as Eddie's friends dragged him away. Barney Tembisa knelt in the corner, there was blood on his mouth and his shoulders shook. Belinda saw tears course down his cheeks, drop from his lips, run down his chest and disappear into the thick hair of his groin. Wolferman got slowly to his feet.

'Always knew you'd turn up at one of my parties, Springer,' he said.

Downstairs, only Belinda was among the crowd who gathered to watch them being taken away. They were marched out by the policemen into the clear early morning light. Wolferman in his shorts and rhino teeshirt and beside him, Tembisa, who for the sake of decency had been draped in the gold patterned bedspread which was far too large for him and dragged behind him like a cloak. Belinda through her pain and fury recognised something absurdly dignified in the progress of this strange couple, the tall, striding figure of Wolferman and beside him the richly swatched, plump figure of his unlikely queen accompanied by their uniformed attendants, yes, that was it, she thought – despite the fact that, as she explained to Malkin and Springer later, she was no monarchist – there was something hideously regal about the procession of Wolferman and his kugel to the waiting police van.

Carnation Butterfly

Eileen Maundy pushed aside her typewriter one bright morning and decided to walk in her garden. It was an admission of defeat. The sticking point was the central character of her new novel, *The Settler's Niece*. The girl in question was Linda who had come to Africa from the Cotswolds to visit her aged, ferocious uncle and who discovered by inexorable, painful illuminations (brilliant and intimate observation of the hairline cracks in the female psyche under pressure being a feature of Maundy's work), that nothing in her foreign English upbringing had prepared her for the racial hatreds which obsessed her old uncle and his country. Her treatment of the initial stages of the girl's painful education was satisfactory. Cool innocence met scalding reality and the resultant burns were revealed with delicate precision. The groundwork was there. But the slow dawning of knowledge was not enough. In this unique land suffering was daily bread, and evil as ordinary as sunshine. That much was clear to Linda. But how to make the fatal knowledge burst in the girl? It needed some perverse act, a violent moment of vision, some brutal unanswerable revelation.

To look at Eileen Maundy was to disbelieve her depth of feeling about such matters. With her fair hair drawn firmly back behind her head, her features neatly angular without being pinched, her small expressive hands and her preference for fine yet unassuming clothes, she looked like a little dressmaker, or as a seamstress might have looked, or a governess. She saw herself, first of all, with just this clarity and she was quite charmingly rueful about the ironies which abounded in the life of herself and her husband, Travers. Their agreeable life, their garden, their double garage and their swimming pool; his work in the personnel department of a big gold mining company; her sense of imminent disaster which suffused all her writing. She had come to terms with the revolution, which, she said in her quiet matter-of-fact voice, would one day put paid to all this, and the neat little hand swept away the garden, the double garage, the swimming pool, and ended in a forefinger on her breast.

All her work explored what someone called 'the bitter fruits of racialism'. Ironic retribution in *Before The Deluge*; the corruptions of power in *Under The Stone*; the virulent gene handed down by the fathers of imperialism and colonialisation which inflamed and infected the lives of their heirs, minutely explored in the famous trilogy: *The Hun At The Gate*, *The Prime Minister's Cousin*, and *Children Of Drought*. 'Invalids of history or muscular hostages?' ran the concluding question in *Under The Stone*. All her work was darkened by this sense of foreboding, of the cataclysm to come, of blood and darkness. '... do you dream of the future?' the mysterious dwarf Loco is asked in *The Hun At The Gate*. 'I have no future, but still I have dreams ...' Loco replies. It was quite simply, as Eileen herself explained it, a wish to make amends. Though others said it should more properly be called a compulsion. The compulsion was given notable expression in the striking short story, *A Spinster's Prayer*, in which a young secretary who has been brutally attacked and stabbed by a blind beggar is shown at the last to have anticipated the attack and even forgiven it:

> *She opened her mouth to tell him she understood but no sound came, only a bubble of blood forced up from her punctured lungs gathered at her lips and broke, like a prayer.*

Keeping his head down Solomon the gardener saw her come out of the house. She was coming to enjoy the garden, the purposeful stride told him that and the towelling robe and the dark glasses. She was coming to the pool, to stretch out for a few hours in the sunshine. Doubtless she would be full of advice. He dug his knees more deeply into the soft turf with a grunt of annoyance and went on cutting the tails of the dahlia tubers which he was planning to plant.

Her garden was stamped with the glistening blue of the pool, its surface flickering back the sunshine as the breeze shifted direction, bouncing the light like a playful child with a mirror making her blink. The wagtails made careful rocking little runs across the lawns. A hedge of roses fenced the garden from the street, the heavy silent suburban street now in mid-morning empty but for the occasional delivery man on his bicycle, pedalling from the pharmacy, grocer, butcher, heavy black bicycles loaded with drugs, meat, flowers. The roses in the hedge were tall, pink mixed with red and flaming orange. As she watched, Solomon let himself out of the gate and busied himself on the pavement.

Solomon obdurate, incorrigible, resisted all suggestions she made with genuine civility and tact. He would not discuss politics with her; declined her invitation to throw off the heavy, sweaty blue overalls and dress in the crisp whites she bought him; preferred not to take his meals with them and even flatly refused her offer to teach him to write. Yet he continued to expect her to bail him out of the police station when he got blind drunk, or was picked up for being without his pass, though she tried often to explain to him that his behaviour played right into the hands of those who exploited him by selling him the drink as well as those who arrested him for suffering from its effects.

From the hedge drifted the plush meaty petals of the blown roses, lying at her feet in fragrant drifts. She touched a large plump yellow rose with an orange tinge, its petals fallen open in the sunshine and in its abandonment to the heat reminding her of the sort of open-mouthed lazy pleasure a dog shows when he lies on his back and spreads his paws and has his belly scratched. The hedge was a good symbol. Perhaps she would have Linda, the old man's niece, facing the hedge just as she did now, thinking it beautiful. It would measure the depth of her deception. For Linda of course couldn't see the thorns for the petals. She couldn't see that it was there not to be admired but to be gone through. Couldn't see that she was no longer in a country of soft, domestic gardens but in the heart of Africa. Yes, Linda would have to go through that hedge. She would have to bleed.

Solomon wished she would come away from his hedge. He had planted a nicely balanced mixture of Hybrid Polyanthus, blending Floribundas, Paulson's Pink, Red Ripples, Floradora and Orange Triumph to make an effective mixture, strong without being garish. It was a good hedge and he was pleased with it, though mildew was something of a problem and he had been careful to dust regularly with powdered sulphur. He caught a glimpse of her legs through the hedge. Soon she would go over to the poolside. She would want her heavy iron chair with the faded cushions; a brute of a thing, difficult to carry. Only that morning he had locked it in the shed.

Eileen Maundy knew Solomon was on the other side of the hedge but she preferred not to speak to him. She couldn't imagine what he was doing outside on the pavement. Stepping even closer to the hedge she peered through its tangle of stem and thorn and saw with a shock that her gardener was down on his knees staring up at her and it was with a stabbing sense of shock and dismay that it occurred to her that he was looking at her legs. She moved away hurriedly, her shock and anger made all the worse by the cool observer within her which both saw and mocked her reaction, the very reaction she herself had deftly pinpointed in various books as the despicable, women's magazines' mish-mash of fears and phobias about the supposed lecherous proclivities of black men. So it was that when she flushed it was with anger and embarrassment.

On his knees behind the hedge Solomon reflected on the

clear signs of mildew he had detected. Regular sulphur dusting should have been enough to control it but then he remembered that rose trees grown in a corridor of the garden where they are exposed to draughts developed mildew rather easily and it occurred to him that the cold east wind that sometimes blew between the high walls and fences of the big houses on their street might well be providing the draught. Perhaps he would try an experiment, perhaps he would burn some paper and gauge the strength of the wind as it passed the hedge.

A column of smoke climbed above the hedge. He was sitting on the ground watching it when she came out of the garden gate.

'Why are you burning paper on the pavement?'

Briefly Solomon contemplated telling her about his theory of the draught but decided against it. He lifted his round, bearded face. He rubbed his jaw. He shrugged. 'I don't know, Madam.'

She ignored the 'Madam', though she had begged him not to use it. 'I don't mind, Solomon, but what do you think the neighbours feel? They see you out here setting fire to pieces of paper and the next thing you know one of them will have called the police. You can't light fires on the pavement.'

Solomon nodded sheepishly.

'Then why do it?'

Again Solomon contemplated telling her of his theory. Instead with his bare feet he stamped out the flames. She had to look away. When the fire was out he followed her into the garden. He chose a corner as far away as possible and began examining a bed of lilies, *lilium regale*; little white trumpets opened their mouths showing their pale yellow throats. On the outside as the flower narrowed to the stem it became suffused with pink. He was pleased with them but when he looked at the next bed containing his snapdragons his heart sank. Several of the flowers evidenced a listless drooping spirit. Here were the unmistakable signs of wilt.

Eileen Maundy noticed his stricken look as he hunched

over the flower-bed and she felt slightly mollified. Perhaps after all he did understand her concern. Solomon, she decided, was all very well at his job. He was devoted to his flowers and kept everything in the garden quite beautifully, but when he got outside that front gate he was absolutely hopeless, he simply didn't understand that out in the world he was a natural victim, prey to the monsters who cruised this vicious society. On reflection she decided that in Solomon's lack of understanding of his position there was a resemblance to the incomprehension of her character, Linda.

Half-hidden in the banks of stocks and sweet peas Solomon watched her making her way to the pool. He felt his mood, already depressed by the discovery of an unmistakable darkening of the lower stems among these flowers which pointed to a bad case of 'black leg', now sinking still further.

Eileen Maundy stepped out of her robe and flung it on the grass. She'd forgotten to wear a hat which was foolish in that heat but she was not going back for it. Beneath her robe she wore a brief, dark blue bikini on which little yellow yachts and seagulls disported themselves. She noticed with some disappointment that the big white iron chair with faded cushions on which she enjoyed lounging by the pool had not been put out but she told herself, half-amused at her own petulance, that she was certainly not going to ask 'Mr Solomon' to fetch it for her. She spread her robe and sat crossed-legged and rubbed suntan oil on to her back and shoulders. Then she stretched herself out in the robe, her cheek on the soft towelling and reaching behind her she undid the straps of her bikini top with a quick deft movement. Out of the corner of her eye she noticed how the grass yellowed at the roots and in the heat heard it ticking faintly like a clock. She smelt the earth, its sweetness strangely interlaced with fumes of chlorine from the pool behind slapping and licking its tiled edges. The sun lay on her back and shoulders.

The breathing woke her, laboured, very close, a shuffling on the grass, then a grunt. Wide-eyed suddenly in the brilliant sunshine she saw before her eyes little hairy cells shimmer and dance. The surface of her skin was hot from the sun but just beneath it the flesh itself was icy and she could feel the oil sliding down her back and sides. Small beads of perspiration crawled in her hair and eyebrows. She could not or perhaps, she told herself with the last vestiges of rationality, she would not move. She would not look. It was closer now, and the breathing louder. A shadow fell across her legs. This was her nightmare, the bloody future. The breathing behind her was loud and quick, she felt his almost unbearable strain. Her mind refused to believe what was happening and yet with her body she knew. With her body she saw him rearing directly above her and she tensed, digging her toes into the turf, waiting for the fall. He reared, high and terrible, and then something heavy hit the grass behind her.

In that moment she made the passage from the clarity of darkest imagination into the brief, banal light of truth, as she was later to describe it to sympathetic friends adding that, paradoxically, her undoing had proved to be the making of her. She had lifted herself literally by the toes and was on her feet running for the house. Later she refused to admit that she had misunderstood or even misapprehended what was happening to her. In a way she insisted she knew, it was not a question of whether the knowledge was right or wrong, it was the knowledge itself that she wanted. It had given her the key to the door that blocked her way to the illumination she had desperately searched for. She had it, as half-naked, fumbling and blinded with tears, she ran into the house and locked the doors and sat down at her desk and without bothering to wipe away the tears that splashed on to the paper, she began to write:

> *The girl at first failed to notice anything but the beauty of the country. Her large bedroom with its high ceilings and the cobwebs in the corner, with the green slatted blinds on the windows which she enjoyed leaving open wide at night. In the morning the sun streamed*

through. There was so much sun. The great garden beyond, its bougainvillaea and its magnolias richly foaming. She barely noticed the gardener whom she regarded as some sort of employee and perhaps imagined he went home at night to his own house with rooms, curtains and carpets on the floor. She looked at Africa but she didn't watch it. She didn't learn to watch others just as they were watching her. So it was that she never watched the gardener in his scratching, delving, harmless trade. She left the windows open behind the closed green curtains as she undressed one evening, let her dress slip to the floor, hooked it on one foot and flicked it across the room in a whirling arc to land on the chair, tongue caught between her teeth in a characteristic grimace of concentration. So it was that hitting her from behind his rush carried her across the room and down on her bed, face pressed down into the pillow, unable to scream, to breathe, to think – knowing only the weight and strength of him, feeling him tear at the last of her clothes, forcing her to bear his weight, to feel fright, pain, then nothing but the crushing, tearing knowledge of Africa around, upon, within her . . .

Solomon stared after the running woman, her breasts bouncing furiously. He watched her disappear into the house and slam the door. He felt a touch of annoyance. The heavy iron chair with which he had staggered across the garden stood uselessly by the poolside. Well, at least now he could get back to work. He'd noticed several of the carnation buds were not opening, their insides burnt out. This was a real blow coming as it did after the other diseases he had detected. The wilt was worst of all. That was incurable. He bent close to the carnations. Some of the plants had spotted leaves and were turning black at the base and dying. Well, he knew he could do something about that. The symptoms were clear, a case of carnation butterfly. He would need a fungicide spray.

Hilton Hits Back

In the matter of orphans, politics is a cruel stepmother. I blame myself entirely for this discovery since it was I who made the family connection in the first place, and for no good reason either. None at all. I've always been one of those rather singular orphans who enjoyed being without parents. I revelled in the so-called disadvantage and, while this made me the odd man out during my time at St Joseph's Home for Boys, up on the Ridge, it paid off when I left St Joe's and went on to university where I found everyone working like crazy to blot out all family connections and transform themselves into orphans. After years of enduring the agony of having the gaps in my life forceably plugged with tatty foster parents and spurious 'aunts', the campus was a liberation and a home-coming. That's why, when I was asked by Hilton van Fölter what I thought of it all, I told him it was a picnic.

Hilton's girl of the month, Sharon, scoffed at Hilton's interest in me. I was, she said, 'a political naif'. And when I looked it up, I decided she was right. When she asked me point blank if I was aware that 'Africans were being crucified on the altar of apartheid'? I had to confess I did not. In fact, I knew nothing at all about Africans. At St Joseph's they were simply the people who polished the floors and got drunk and stabbed each other during wild parties in the servants' quarters on Saturday nights and their screams in the night were merely a component of the African soundscape, blending with the shrilling crickets and the frogs. Of course, in my first six weeks on campus, before I met Hilton, I began to get a political education: I became dimly aware that apartheid was bad; it made black people suffer and it was up to us to oppose it. You could say I was developing the usual vague, liberal leanings. I'd never been on a protest march and never attended a mass student meeting. But then commerce students didn't much go in for that sort of thing. I got the impression that it was more the province of the 'arts' crowd who were led by the hard men in the student radical movement, and the hard men were led by Hilton van Fölter. All this changed when Hilton recruited me for what he called my great advantage, my 'radical orphanhood'.

Hilton was the old man of the campus and the champion fighter for racial equality. No one knew *how* old he was, though I've heard his age put at twenty-seven. Personally, I feel that's rather exaggerated. No one knew what course he was taking and if you asked them, people in the know muttered something vague about 'honours', in politics perhaps. Others said it was social anthropology. He went to no lectures though he could be seen everywhere on the campus, a bulky, untidy figure in a cracked panama, flapping along in old grey flannels and torn sandals over the edges of which his black, uncut toenails protruded like the eaves of a roof. I'd never met anyone who cared so little about how he looked. Fresh out of the orphanage as I was, where darning, patching and polishing, turning shirt collars and dropping hems did more than keep clothes on the back, they stitched the world together, and proud of my first team school tie and blue barathea blazer, a present from the Rector, overcome that a boy from 'the Home' should have won a full scholarship to university, I looked on Hilton's extravagant sloppiness as an illness, a destructive disease, the deliberate murder of the duty to turn out looking clean and neat in public, drummed into us at St Joseph's as being the poor child's only defence in a sharp-eyed, mercenary world.

When Hilton one day collared me on the campus and

talked politics, furiously fanning himself with his panama in the sweltering heat, the mechanical summer sunshine that seemed to switch itself on every morning and rose to an unvarying solar whine, shrillest at noon and burning through the afternoon skies like white ash, I found myself turning my face away when he spoke in case I picked up a trace of his disease. I overcame this prejudice during the mammoth seminar on Marxist policies he gave me over the next weeks and was soon breathing in the air he breathed out as if I'd been doing it all my life though I never could turn out on campus looking anything but clean and neat. As it happened, I was to pay dearly for this.

'This may look like a picnic to you, tootling around the place in collar and tie like a Jehovah's Witness on house calls, but I invite you to look again. What you are seeing is a battlefield.'

Obediently, I peered about me at the bright, noisy campus crowded with sports cars and motor bikes: I saw girls in bikinis shining like buttered kippers under their suntan oil, who lay soaking up the sun around the ornamental fountains; I watched as others in tiny shorts or shocking pink ski-pants strolled between lectures arm in arm with white-coated medics or stocky engineers in baggy khaki shorts and traditional thick woollen socks. I saw a scratch team from my commerce class score against a team of grey-suited lawyers in a game of touch rugby beside the swimming pool. I said I thought much of the fighting must be going on beneath the surface.

'It's a war to the death,' Hilton assured me. 'We are out to smash the system. This means hitting our parents. That's tough. But the old wrinklies are usually the system's first line of defence.'

I noticed how many girls waved at Hilton who flapped his panama in return with a careless flourish. His reputation as an 'older' man and a political wildman was a potent attraction. They said he was so popular that he took his women on a strict rota and limited himself to one a month.

'I'm an orphan.'

'Really? I had to fight for my freedom. You're one up on me there. Tragedy aside, it's a headstart. Stay lucky like that always.'

Hilton's own struggle against his parents was campus legend and every freshman heard it about two minutes after arriving. Hilton's family were rich. His father was a pure capitalist who ran an airline and sent his son up to university to become a dentist. One afternoon, in the middle of a lab practical on elementary exodontics, he collapsed at his bench. Some said he faked it but Hilton swore he had had a vision of a new society based on racial justice and equity, 'probably on a par with St Paul's, if not higher,' was how his girl of the month, Sharon, explained it to me. Anyway the upshot of it was that he disowned his father, gave up his silk shirts, his Dunhill pipe and his cut-price holiday flights to places like Bermuda, dropped out of dentistry and enrolled in the course on 'Politics and Existence' given by the legendary neo-Hegelian, B. F. E. Lestrade, 'Buffy' to his friends and adoring students, until the sad business of the Registrar's nephew gave his enemies their chance to hound him from his job and the country, a ruined man, though retaining to the last enough of his stinging humour to tell a brash reporter who asked sneeringly about his plans at a press conference organised by Hilton and a few staunch admirers that he was off to Hamburg where he planned to open a male brothel. At the time of his vision, when he booted dentures into touch, Hilton's reading didn't extend beyond, say, Black's *Operative Dentistry*. Buffy Lestrade introduced him to Marx and the rest is history.

'Buffy's father, believe it or not,' Hilton told me with a grin during my new political education, 'was actually a semi-professional soccer player. Can you credit it? He played on the right wing for Callies. Imagine the leap Buffy had to make to get out of that hole! It led him to develop his theory about the vital need to maintain the split between child and parent as the way to kill off old, engrained racial thinking in this country. Of course, most kids at university go through the rejection stage; a year killing off parents, a year adjusting to freedom, a year of political struggle and then, sadly, the inevitable degree, a job in a mining house and return to the family fold. Buffy saw that we had to really work at widening the generation gap. "Radical orphanhood" – to speak in Lestradian terms – now that's what we're after in the progressive movement. And that's where you score. You're a natural.'

In our two-week, walking seminar Hilton told me about the economic basis of racialism, the institutionalising of alienation, the one-dimensional, or what he called the 'flat-map' distortion of African history, and the dialectics of protest. It was, he confessed modestly, no more than theoretical structure. Even the protest marches and demonstrations were theoretical. This was the stage the struggle had reached. He looked towards the day when we'd move beyond the battle of words and begin to act, to seize the chance of genuinely authentic existence, to make something *real* happen.

Stencilled on the side of the old rucksack Hilton used as a book bag was a row of policeman's helmets, set out like fighter-pilots chalk up their 'kills'. Each helmet stood for an arrest. The number of his arrests – some twelve to date – on demonstration marches was the toast of the illicit late-night parties held in safe houses in the suburbs where radical black and white students met, mingled, drank and danced together. I never got to any of those. Well, I did go once, on the night before my first protest march, with a rather plain girl called Dodie from my elementary statistics class who shared my liberal yearnings and had a car to boot. But we couldn't find parking. At least, not until it was too late, because the place was solid with limousines for blocks around. We finally made it as the party was packing up. Nobody told me you were supposed to get there late for safety's sake, but not too late or otherwise the student cars jammed the streets for blocks around and the security police who always followed them and invariably gate-crashed the party pretending to be drunken accountants, or radical theology students, would grab what little parking remained.

'The really old hands form lift-clubs,' Sharon revealed pityingly when I told her about it. She was in second-year sociology, blonde, terribly tense, so painfully thin that the bony hollows on each side of her neck looked as if they would have held half a cup of water apiece. She had this habit of turning her head away while she was speaking and looking at you out of the corner of her eye. She was the sort of girl who carried her conscience in a holster. 'And what's your field?' She glanced at my barathea blazer and tie.

'First-year commerce. I've never been on a march before. Shall I nip back to my rooms and change?'

She gave me a look of remorseless sympathy. 'We all have our cross. No, don't change. It's strictly come as you are.'

We had assembled to pick up our banners and posters for the march on the central police station in town. All the protest material had been made by the girls of the Student Christian Association under Sharon's direction. There was a fine selection of placards, many with hand-embroidered slogans, others stiff with red ribbon rosettes; some were even done in batik and others stamped with original African wood-cuts. Hilton went to a lot of trouble choosing something suitable for me.

'As this is your first time, I think you ought to be allowed to make a bit of a show. What about this one? The reference is especially apt. I like my material to have point and communicate fast. Can't mince words. Most of the crowd who see our marches are as thick as two planks. You will march up front and tell the so-called electorate exactly what we think of the people they've voted into power and I hope it jolly well stings.'

That's how I came to lead the march of several hundred students, carrying a placard bearing a big, grainy blown-up photograph of the prime minister over the challenging question: *A Vote for Barabbas?* The police were to take strong exception to this and, truth be told, I had to agree with them. Personally, I've always considered our prime minister looked more like a sinister medieval pontiff. I suppose it's the veiny nose and the sunken eyes that give the impression, and of course, the little shining cap of hair combed flat strengthens the papal look. The eyes are sunken and of so light a blue they seem almost colourless, like drying water-holes, receding into their sockets leaving the surrounding banks of flesh seamed and folded like river sand. All in all, a profligate pope more likely to be given to highly individual vices behind consistory doors than petty thievery. But there you are – Hilton van Fölter said it must be Barabbas and Barabbas it was.

I offered to take off my tie.

'Do you feel too dressed?' Hilton asked. '*Per contra.* We want that, I think. It's the shocking difference, you see, between the look of you, as it were, stiff and formal and clean, and the poster you're carrying.' For some reason he was wearing an old leather flying helmet and enormous gauntlets. 'Who would imagine such a conventional guy – ' he smashed a fist into his palm – 'could pack such a punch!'

Sharon looked sceptical. 'Don't you think, Hilt, that pushing him out front, especially with *that* placard, is risky? It makes him look so, well, prominent. The cops could just possibly home in on him. And this is his first time. A baby accountant in his blazer and tie.'

'But that's just it! There is something symbolic about it, something vestal, even. Picture it. The virgin out front, pure and undefiled. Yet he carries – and here we score, he's carrying this profane message challenging, attacking the onlookers. Do you realise that were it not for their uniforms the cops would be onlookers too? Don't forget they're also human, just as open to the force of symbols, just as liable to be taken by our street theatre. Who knows, one day we might score with them. As for handling himself, remember I've taught this boy all I know.'

'And he couldn't have had a better teacher – but it's still all theory.'

Hilton bridled. 'For God's sake, Shar – theory! This fellow's a professional orphan. He knows more about holding out against the old guard than you and I put together.' He turned on me. 'Right?'

139

Of course I had no option then. The honour of orphans was at stake. 'Right.'

'Besides,' Hilton gave his famous hurt, modest half-smile, and touched her cheek soothingly, 'remember we're up there with him. If they do jump, I think we all know who they're likely to land on.'

Sharon melted. She lifted a flap of helmet and kissed his ear. 'Okay Hilt. I believe.'

Hilton briefed us then, cupping his gloved hands so his voice boomed. 'I won't say much. Most of you know the ropes but for the benefit of newcomers I'll just go over salient points. Once we reach the police station sit down. Placards must be legible at all times. I'll make a short speech. The cops will then read the riot act and order us to disperse. Please, this is very important, *please*, don't move until I give the signal. Perfect timing is crucial. It's important that we leave after the warning but *before* they charge and judging that is a delicate matter. Keep your eyes on me. When we withdraw, do so in a body, with placards – and I can't repeat this too often – placards held high, banners taut. Thank you.'

I hadn't imagined the police might turn nasty. It gave a slight tremor.

'But what happens if they pick on us?'

'Sit tight,' Sharon advised. 'A good rule of thumb is – if in doubt, don't hit back. It only makes matters worse.'

'Just keep your eyes on me,' Hilton repeated, sadly, wearily, his face moonishly grave in the circle of the flying helmet. 'And if you see them land on me, don't panic. You're not here to save me. You're expressing solidarity with the oppressed and don't forget it. Besides, I'm more or less prepared for anything they may throw at me. Comes of practice.'

'Practice makes perfect,' Sharon said quietly. I laughed.

'It's not a joke.' She was cross. 'Hilton has borne the worst of the police attacks. He's been hurt so often, I sometimes think he is trying to perfect his life through suffering. Like a saint.'

We marched in threes. I was placed between Hilton and Sharon and we led the waving column out of the university grounds under the great arch, surmounted by a bronze giantess with her arm thrown around the neck of a young doe signifying 'Hope in Pursuit of Peace', past the fountain opposite the main gates where a granite lioness, symbolising Mother Africa, suckled four identical cubs representing the four major racial groups each with its sacred right to separate but equal freedoms, and into the heavy traffic moving towards town. The importance of my position gave me butterflies and I wished I'd eaten before leaving. I noticed that several students had brought along packed lunches. Old hands.

We snaked along the side of the road in a fairly disciplined column, which was something of an achievement because we came in for a lot of stick from passing motorists who seemed to delight in driving dangerously close, hooting, pulling monkey faces and jeering at us. The beefy driver of a blue Zephyr slowed down to a snail's pace and rolled down his window. Hilton ignored him. Leaning on a freckled, meaty, muscled arm stuck on the door-jamb, he advised us to get our hair cut.

'Fascist,' Hilton retorted, not missing a step.

'Bloody commie.'

'Rockspider.'

The beefy man acknowledged this traditional insult by switching into his native Afrikaans with a terrible oath about Hilton's mother's womb.

'My mother is Africa,' Hilton replied, also in Afrikaans.

'Looking at you – she's been sleeping around.' And he roared away.

'Thanks for the compliment!' Hilton shrieked after him. The straps of his flying helmet danced about his ears and we all cheered wildly and it felt more like a picnic than ever.

The central police station was a tall skyscraper that could be mistaken for one of the banks or insurance companies which surrounded it. We sat down on the pavement and Hilton made a speech calling for an end to racism and segregated buses; I seem to remember he demanded also that the municipality made liquor licences available to student canteens and ended by quoting Abe Lincoln who had once said that for evil to succeed it was enough that good men remained silent. A burst of rowdy applause greeted this compliment which Hilton acknowledged with a confident thumbs-up. I'm afraid that I got rather carried away at this point and jumped up calling for three cheers for Hilton. Sharon shushed me.

The police faced us with water-hoses. The station commander, red-faced, irritable, speaking through a megaphone, warned us that the demonstration was illegal. Hilton responded with the flurry of sign language indicating that we should sit down in the road and keep quiet. When we had settled down the commander, after much smoothing of his grey drooping moustache, read us the riot act, or rather he quoted it from memory in a stilted way, like an actor with a hazy grasp of his lines. I noticed how carefully everything was staged, it was a sort of play in which everyone knew their parts. If we did not leave quietly, the commander warned, we would be dispersed with all necessary force. Again, Hilton's eloquent gestures told us to sit tight. The police held a huddled conference and a large constable came deliberately down the steps to where we sat stiff and proud at the head of our brave demonstration. I felt Hilton tense beside me. He foresaw another helmet on his book bag. Instead, blow me down if the cop doesn't grab me and demand that I go with him. When I refused he grabbed me under the elbows and began heaving me up the steps. Hilton jumped up furious and tried to stop him. This clearly wasn't in the script. Sharon shrieked that they had no right to arrest me. Hilton said that this was my first time. Sharon explained that I was 'only a commerce student'. The constable put me down, drew his truncheon and hit Hilton hard and low, in the groin, I think, because he dropped like a stone. Sharon screamed that they had murdered him. Then the cops with the hoses turned them on full force, working with a terrible nonchalance; they might have been hosing down their driveways on a hot Sunday afternoon and in about two minutes flat they'd cleared the road.

Once they got me inside the police seemed to lose interest. Certainly, I wasn't much of a catch. It had been the poster they were after. Sharon had been right. After examining it mournfully, the commander pointed out its inaccuracy. If I'd compared the prime minister with, say, Genghis Khan, or Hitler, that would have been typical student abuse. But to compare him with a common thief, and with this particular thief, was beyond the pale. The desk sergeant, a young man called Hattingh, said blasphemy made him want to vomit. He demanded my first-team tie as well as my watch and spare cash; on the grounds that a prisoner had recently hung himself with his long-johns and he didn't want me getting ideas. But I noticed he spoke without much hope.

The constable who arrested me took me down to the cells in the basement. The feeling seemed to be that since he'd pulled me in, I was his problem. His name was Swanepoel, Swannie to his colleagues. The lock-ups weren't too bad, if rather dirty, painted in government green with double bunks, a slop pail and one small window high up and heavily barred, the thick, greenish glass bleary with dust.

'What gives you people the right to trample all over people's religious beliefs?' Swanepoel demanded.

I saw my chance and spoke to him at some length, and rather well too, if I may say so myself, about the economic basis of racialism. He heard me out in silence and when I finished he spat carefully into a corner of my cell and said that I hadn't answered his question.

But I wasn't giving in that easily. 'What gives you the right to trample all over black people?'

He lifted one boot then the other with studied concentration. 'Black people,' he called softly, 'come out, little black people, Old Swannie's not going to hurt you.'

Two could play that game. I sat on my bunk and took a foot in my hand and examined the sole of my shoe minutely while he looked on, puzzled. 'Not a trampled principle in sight,' I shook my head sadly. 'Not a trace.'

He took off his cap and squinted at me suspiciously. Then he laughed. Seeing him there twisting his cap in his big hands until the grommet popped, with his toothy grin and close-cropped blond hair, it came as a shock to realise that he couldn't have been much older than me.

'You've got me there, Barabbas. That's the trouble with playing with words. I'm tired of words. I want action. It's time something happened. Something real.'

'What do you mean *real*? What's more real than *apartheid*?'

He put on his cap and shrugged. 'Trouble with you guys is that you're so damn superior.'

That really stung. 'Listen, I'm not superior. I'm in jail for not being superior and for wanting to smash the system.'

He grinned again. 'Cheap talk. It's no great shakes to be in jail, you know. You're too stuck up to see you couldn't smash your way out of a paper bag.'

'And who am I supposed to be superior to?'

He winked. 'Folks like me,' he said, and he was gone.

An investigation of my cell brought a joyful discovery. If I climbed on to the top bunk I could reach the window bars and haul myself up to the grimy pane and get a blurred, ankle-level view of the street directly outside the station. I could hold myself up only for a few minutes at a time but it was enough. It was from this vantage point that I watched the second demonstration later that day.

A column of students, mostly the same lot who had marched that morning, carrying new banners and placards, led the way and formed up on the pavement across the road from the police station. Here was a heavy iron gate barring the entrance to an alley which ran between two buildings. A naked man bent double under a cross made of some blond wood staggered up to the iron gate. It was Hilton, of course. A working party lowered the cross to the ground and when they raised it up again he was fixed to it and the cross was bound to the gate with ropes, or perhaps chains. Hilton was not naked as I'd thought but he wore a pair of tiny black and yellow, fake-leopard skin underpants. A woman in flowing black, and heavily veiled, pushed her way through the crowd and took up a position at the foot of the cross and I knew this silent, shrouded mourner was she of the bird-bath shoulders, Hilton's girl of the month, Sharon. I also knew that Hilton was going for broke. My arrest must have been the last straw. In the face of his advice to me, Hilton had decided to hit back.

Then there were police everywhere, charging furiously with batons drawn. It was like watching a silent film. For a few minutes the air flocked with torn posters and flying caps and bristled with sticks as the cops laid about them. Some removed their heavy leather belts and whipped the demonstrators. The dogs followed, huge Alsatians bounding ahead of their handlers, straining at their short leads and making snarling rushes at the few students left on their feet. One of the dogs leaped at the sorrowing Sharon and ripped her mantilla from her head: I saw her face for an instant, white and furious, before she too went down. The cowed students were carted away crying and clutching legs and arms where the dogs whipped to a frenzy by their near-hysterical handlers had taken hold so fiercely of a calf or wrist that they had to be beaten off with truncheons. It was over quickly. In a minute and a half or so, the pavement was clear except for shredded posters, one high-heeled shoe, a few crumpled banners, a spreading pool of something, blood perhaps, or simply orange juice spilled from the smashed flask some thoughtful mother had packed for her child that morning, and, of course, old Hilton luckily too high for the dogs. One particularly demented Alsatian wouldn't give up, leaping for him again and again and falling back, only to leap again like he was attached to some invisible spring yanking him upwards, and snapping at Hilton's bare soles as if he were a treed cat, until his handler pulled the beast away.

Swanepoel came back. He glanced up at the window. 'From your little paw marks I see you've discovered the peephole. Well, what do you think of the latest gimmick?'

I told him it wasn't a gimmick. 'I know Hilton. This is serious. He's out to sacrifice himself.' I told him about

Hilton's impatience with theory. This was precisely the action that he, Swanepoel, had been waiting for. For good measure I told him about institutional alienation. I quoted Lestrade on radical orphanhood. 'Hilton has been frustrated too long. Now he's going to make something happen.'

He looked pained. 'How does walking around in your underpants help? This is only one step up on your placard, Barabbas. Another joke, another game.'

'Game? I saw the game you played out there. The dogs, the sticks . . .'

He nodded gloomily. 'Exactly. Toys. If we'd been serious we should have shot the lot.'

Anger made me reckless. 'Why didn't you?'

He stared at me furiously. 'How could we? We're all on the same side. We're all so damn, so damn – ' he searched for a word and when he got it out I knew he'd been listening to my lectures, but knowing it made it worse ' – *booshwah*! I mean – take that cross. What's it made from?'

It was my turn to shrug. 'What does it matter?'

He grabbed the iron bedstead and rattled it angrily. 'You've gone to sleep in your cage, man! Of course it matters. It's made of pine, see? And do you know what happens to local pine when it gets wet? It warps, natch. A shower of rain and that piece of lucky-packet carpentry will fall down. But then it wasn't built to last. That mad bimbo van Fölter doesn't plan to be up there long. The way he had calculated it, we'd foam at the mouth and arrest him – but if not, well then his friends'll nip along after dark and take him down.'

'That's a lie.' I showed all the dignity I could muster. 'Besides, how are his friends going to help him? You've got them all locked up.'

He gave a bitter little laugh, half a sob. 'Oh yes, we locked them up. We packed them, see? Six to a four-man pen licking their wounds, kids retching, old hands up on the top bunk because they know the air's a bit fresher there when the slop pails begin to fill up, when kabam! the usual invasion hits us. Usual but for its size, that is: mommies and daddies, hundreds of them it seemed, fancy folk, togged up to the nines in gold trouser-suits and hacking-jackets and navy blazers, just like yours there, and as per usual crying and shouting all at once and the road outside the station is jammed solid with their cars – oh, I've seen it a hundred times, only tonight it was virtually a riot. News has spread, you see, that we'd put in the dogs. Some parents arrived with bandages, entire damn first-aid kits, and one old lady, tall blonde in a black mink, thick as thatch, comes in, cool as you please and tells the desk sarge he's got to clear the road outside otherwise the private ambulance she's ordered can't get through!' Swanepoel gave a shout of laughter at the memory; he teetered between horrified incredulity and outright amusement and clearly enjoyed it. He leaned an elbow casually against the top bunk muttering and shaking his head at the amazing memory. 'Well, I went outside with the sarge to take a look. Jeez! I tell you I haven't seen so many Rovers and Jags and Lincoln Continentals since I drew duty as parking attendant at the governor-general's garden party there by the Union Buildings – actually I was lumbered, on account of old Wynand Ferreira, who was supposed to be my relief, having to play an away-game that Saturday, for Police Seconds against Benomi Pirates – anyway, as I was saying, there's this crowd of idle rich queuing to bail their brats out of the lock-up, poor little Doreen, and darling Julius who is delicate, and baby Stuart who never in his life did anything worse than steal sweets from the corner cafe, and boys will be boys, and you're only young once, etcetera . . .' He sighed and stomped around the cell muttering to himself and plunging his hands deep into his pockets and grabbing the linings so that his heavy serge turn-ups lifted inches above his boots. 'That's typical! Par for the course. You nice liberal guys go around being kind to Africans, stirring up trouble, having more fun than an intervarsity rugby match and then at the end of the day, when all hell breaks loose, off you go, home to silk sheets and Mommy's cooking, leaving old Swannie to hold the fort? He turned on me suddenly. 'Why are you still here? Why haven't your folks been along looking for their little Barabbas?'

I felt deserted, wretched and my voice wouldn't rise above a whisper. 'I don't have any people. I'm from the boy's home. St Joseph's – you know, the one on the Ridge.'

Swanepoel smashed his fist into his palm. 'You're an orphan? Who is going to bail you out? Without bail, you'll stay here until the trial. The others will also come to court but they'll pay admission of guilt fines. Can you pay? If you can't – then zap! – straight into jail.'

I tried to keep a grip on myself. 'That's what you want. Look on the bright side,' I suggested in a voice made hideously squeaky by fear. 'We haven't all walked out on you. I'm still here. So is Hilton.'

'For how long?'

'To the end.'

Swanepoel smiled a sarcastic smile that pulled his lips into a thin, tight loop, like one of those rubber seals for stopping preserve jars. 'You believe that, Barabbas?'

I nodded.

'Did it ever occur to you that maybe you aren't an orphan after all. Maybe your folks simply gave you away because you were too stupid to keep?'

After he'd gone I climbed up to the window. Hilton hung heavily and the last of the sunset was flaring in his hair. It would have been very dramatic if it hadn't been clear, even through the foggy glass, how much he was suffering. Even with the useful little standing support at the foot of the cross the strain on his muscles and circulation must have been excruciating. His head lolled rather dreadfully and his knees were turned out and bent as if he was trying to draw them up, but the ropes or straps stopped that. I'm ashamed to confess I was reassured. He was still there, like me, hanging on.

When Swanepoel arrived with supper of sausages and mash, and stood over me while I forced it down he was suddenly a changed man. He pointed out that by covering my slop pail with my blazer I would 'keep down household odours', and he was quite dismayingly friendly. He made me eat every last bit because, he said, he didn't want me 'wasted away' when I got out. He relished my look of goofy astonishment. My God, but he lapped it up! I didn't care. I begged him to explain. Grinning, he took off his cap, sat down on the bunk beneath me. He told me he had every reason to believe, to hope, that Hilton wouldn't last the night.

'But how do you know?'

'Been out there with the police surgeon. Old van Fölter has got the spastic jitters. The doc says he'll croak by morning – of something fancy . . . car-box-y-hemia.' He said it lovingly.

'What's that?'

'Oh, cramps, breathing problems, collapse – that's just about the order of play. But don't ask me, I'm no medical man.'

'I just thought since you knew the name . . .'

'I'm a policeman,' Swanepoel said with dignity. 'We're trained to remember details like that. Anyway rejoice Barabbas, because I bought your theory that he's in this for keeps. We'll seal off the street – for his own protection, of course. We'll say members of the public, outraged by his behaviour, have made death threats. So no one can get near him. Then by tomorrow morning we're all laughing. Van Fölter gets to be a hero like he's always wanted. We get van Fölter. The commander loves it.'

I looked at his shining eyes. In an awful way his enthusiasm was catching. 'You've got it all sewn up, then.'

He nodded firmly. 'I think so. The commander also has his doubts, mind you, he's never pushed anything as far as this before. Not used to working things through to conclusions, you might say, guys croaking in the streets, and that – but to his credit, he's prepared to let me have a go – "nothing ventured, nothing win, old Swannie," was the way he put it. And if we pull it off, it'll be a feather in his cap, a big catch, van Fölter dead that is. As a university man, you get the thinking behind this.'

I did. 'If you land the big fish, you can afford to throw the little one back?'

'It must be wonderful to have an education,' he said.

He showed no sign of wanting to leave. In fact, he settled back on the lower bunk with a contented sigh and stretched out his legs and startled me by actually asking me to tell him some more about 'all the political mumbo-jumbo'. He insisted I called him Swannie – at least, 'between ourselves'. What could I do? I told him about the 'flat-map' theory of African history, I told him about the dialectics of protest. But I must confess my heart wasn't in it. If he noticed my lack of fervour he didn't mention it and when I'd finished he thanked me, jumped up, punched me playfully on the shoulder.

'You're a lucky guy, Barabbas. Not only have you got all the theory of this business absolutely pat, but you're going to experience a bit of action for a change. You're going to see the making of a martyr of the revolution. At long bloody last we're going to see a little action around here.'

'You really think Hilton is going to die?' It wasn't clear to me whether I asked the question for information or reassurance.

He favoured me with a large, careful wink. 'He'd better. We all depend on it.'

I'd like to say I never closed an eye that night. In fact, I went out like a light and slept like a baby. It might seem heartless, but, the truth is, I believed in Hilton – I really believed. Accordingly, it took me some time to get my mind into gear when, early the next morning, with the cold light of dawn pushing through the dirty window, Swanepoel shook me awake.

'Sorry, hey, Barabbas. They sent in the cavalry.' His smile was ghastly.

'Has Hilton been moved?'

He shrugged. 'We refused to lift a finger. The commander told them they'd have to make their own arrangements. Why don't you shin up to the window and take a look?'

Through the dirty glass I watched the whole thing. Hilton

slumped on his cross with his head still lolling dreadfully. He didn't move. Perhaps he was dead. I rather hoped that he was dead. Death seemed infinitely preferable to any other destination just then. A squad of black workmen, shouldering assorted tools in neat blue overalls, swung into view, two abreast, moving at the double and behind them, shouting out the step, loped a white man in khaki shorts and a broadbrimmed bush hat with a leopard skin band that matched Hilton's underpants. Clearly he was the foreman and he drove them to the foot of the cross where they marked time with great precision.

'They're about to move him,' I told Swanepoel.

'Who've they got?'

'A gang of workmen. Professionals. Plenty of tools. And big red letters stitched on their backs. DPR, I think.'

He grunted. 'Parks department. The pull those people have got is bloody incredible. I mean who else could just rustle up a working party from the Department of Parks and Recreation at the crack of dawn? It's not right. Makes you realise they've got the country in their pocket. Makes you think.'

The foreman halted his workmen, produced a folding camp stool and sat down while someone ran up a ladder and gave Hilton a quick inspection. There was a hasty conference. I guessed that the chains or whatever had been used to secure him to the gates presented a problem. A man was despatched and returned with a hacksaw. Minutes later the chains fell away and the cross with its deathly pale burden was lowered gently on to the shoulders of the workmen who formed up to take its weight, three beneath the upright and three along the horizontal traverse bar, and then they were off, stamping a right foot in unison as they went and singing, in the way Africans will when a group must work with precision at some heavy job, with the foreman trailing behind, folding stool slung over his shoulder.

'I made a plea to the commander. The bimbo in the underpants wants to die. Let him, I said. The orphan wants to leave. Let him.' Swanepoel sat next to me and patted my shoulder clumsily. 'Make a stand sir, I said, it's your choice.

'He just looked at me with these cow eyes and says: I got no choice, Swannie. Van Fölter's girl did the damage – the one all dressed up like a Spanish granny in black veils and whatall. Late last night she slipped past the constables sealing off the street. Don't ask me how. They got her but she had time to get close to the cross. She swears she heard the crazy bimbo talking to himself. She says he was asking for his old man. So she hotfoots it to daddy and he rolls up and leans on the commander. I mean, he's some big-shot on the airways. He's got government connections as long as my arm. He appeals to the commander as a family man, father to father, y'know. Made me want to puke. Hilton has always been a high-spirited lad, he said, and they have had their little tiffs, as witness the fact that the little beggar hasn't spoken a word to his old pa for donkey's years. He offers a deal – let the commander allow his son's release and he will personally guarantee that the foolish young chap goes away, out of the country, for a long holiday – some place overseas, I don't know where – Belgium? The Bahamas?'

'Bermuda?'

'That's it. I'm sorry, Barabbas. Things don't look too good for you. I've thought about it, inasmuch as an uneducated bugger like me can be said to think – and things don't look too good. So far as I can see there is only one bit of hope . . .'

I felt a faint, foolish surge of hope. 'For me?'

He laughed gently. 'You're joking. I admire a man who can keep his sense of humour at a time like this. No, for me. Like I've told you, I've had enough games. I've had enough of nothing happening.'

I turned over on the bunk and buried my face in the harsh mattress and hoped very much Swanepoel would go away. But I heard him walking around the cell clicking his fingers.

'No, this hope of mine has to do with the talks we been having, you and me. Private like. Now, just look on the bright side, as you told me. Or, put another way, not one door opens but another closes, or something like that.

Anyway, what I'm saying is that you having to stay on here now, maybe for ages still, is just what the doctor ordered. I mean, like I said last night – you've got the theory and I want to see action. Right? So being cooped up like this, the *two* of us, you are perfectly placed to tell me all I want to know about how to do it.'

The guy was driving me crazy. 'Dammit man – tell you what?'

He came over and put his lips right close to my ear. 'How to smash the system,' he said.

So, for what it was worth, I told Swanepoel what I knew. He listened very carefully and then proceeded to tell me what had to be done if meaning was to be restored to words such as 'radical' and 'orphan' and the movement towards reality to begin. Soon afterwards he arranged that I should be released on bail which he paid, a fatherly thing to have done though he was too discreet to mention that fact, a tactfulness for which I was grateful. A week later, charges against me were dropped.

I went back to the campus. Swannie stayed in the force. On the face of it nothing seemed to have changed. Admittedly, once back at university it would be fair to say that because of my experiences, I cut something of a figure though I hasten to add that I did nothing to encourage the fame which association with Hilton's last days had brought upon me. In fact I did everything possible to emphasise the great difference between our life styles and political views. I attended classes religiously, passed my examinations, wore my hair very short and never appeared in public without a jacket and tie. It would be fair to say that I was a model student. I insisted on a similar reticence among my followers; one might be known, but on no account was one to be noticeable. Of course, no one had the least idea that I had attracted followers. No one knew we existed, but our group grew steadily and numbered some two dozen after a period of careful and highly selective recruitment. Swannie's cell at the station was growing too and more and more of the junior officers had, as he put it, 'come across'. The third force which Swannie had planned for was growing. The movement towards reality was underway. Sooner or later something was really going to happen.

Hilton was gone but not forgotten. In his absence his followers rallied around Sharon on whom his mantle had fallen. They still talked of revolution, of sacrifice, of solidarity with the oppressed, or praxis and the flat-map theory of history and sometimes even of Buffy Lestrade. But mostly they simply talked. Sharon was making the most of things. She encouraged the belief that Hilton was watching over them like a dead hero among the gods in Valhalla. She had been heard to compare herself with the widow of the assassinated President Allende of Chile. Hilton himself continued to recuperate in Bermuda and nothing had been heard from him since he left.

Hilton's father continued friendly with the station commandant and that was how Swannie heard that his son was secretly planning to return, a reformed character, full of good sense and the right political attitudes. It was decided that we should immediately hold a special session of our action committee. An important decision was taken. Swanepoel and his people were to prepare the station hot-heads for a most violent demonstration. My followers were to whip up the campus in anticipation of a triumphal entry into the city. In this, I think it fair to say, we excelled ourselves. A few hours after we broke the news, Hilton's return was being compared by his delirious followers to the triumphal entry into Jerusalem. Sharon, ever quick to learn, decided the comparison was so apt that she went out and hired a donkey.

When Hilton stepped off the plane from Bermuda his followers mobbed him and having imagined he was slipping into the country unnoticed, he was shaken by the tumultuous reception. He turned very pale and this, together with his offwhite tropical suit and dirty cream silk shirt, gave him a wonderfully ethereal air when he was hauled down the gangway from the plane and seated on the donkey for his triumphal entry into the city. I don't think he knew what was happening to him. My people moved amongst the disciples distributing palms. When Hilton protested it was taken for modesty and his hysterical friends wept and beat their breasts and waved their palms in a fury of adoration. We had planned the route carefully and the march took Hilton past the sites of many demonstrations he'd led in the old days, arriving finally at the police station where Sharon, dressed in full widow's weeds, dropped the donkey's lead and laid a wreath. The policemen inside the station looked on in a fury. The disciples screamed and fainted. Hilton was persuaded to address them. Trembling he was helped down from the ass. The instant his feet touched the ground all hell broke loose. His followers tried to rip down the heavy cast-iron gates across the mouth of the sacred alley. The police came down on them like wolves.

It was never known who struck Hilton down. Each side blamed the other. The fact was he was dead. Having survived his crucifixion, his resurrection finished him. He'd gone to a place where his father's connections could not touch him. Hilton had finally hit back. Reality was beginning to set in.

The Fall of the British Empire

Having been introduced to the boys by the headmaster, Mr Sessi stands silent for a moment with a look both bright and pleasant on his face. He is the first Sierra Leonian we have seen, certainly the first to whom we can put a name, and we gaze back with interest. To the students slouched in their uncomfortable chairs, Mr Sessi is familiar only by the colour of his skin, the prevalence of which, in all its shades, is deplored across the Midlands even if seldom seen in such blackness, a special item of interest in Mr Sessi's case. So many people have said to me: 'We used to have very good relations with the coloured people – but, of late, we've been feeling rather overwhelmed.' On such occasions, I never know what to answer, so I nod and look away, which is often taken as an expression of sympathy. Since I am known as a South African, I don't suppose it could be taken any other way.

To the boys who comprise his audience, Mr Sessi could not be more remote in his origins, in the case of his mind and the exoticism of his perspiration, had he come from the dark side of the moon. These boys are fourteen years old, the Easter School-Leavers the staff call them; to the school they are known as the dum-dums. Their clothes are carefully chosen to show that they regard themselves as pretty tough, showing a lot of denim, carefully faded and raggy in the right places, and heavy boots, studded at heel and toe. In the matter of his foreignness, I have the advantage over them because Mr Sessi comes from Black Africa which is geographically close to South Africa, and geography is my subject. That is to say, I'm paid to teach it. In actual fact, I spend lesson times fending off diversionary questions about Zulu chiefs and witchdoctors, but no matter.

Sierra Leone, named by the Portuguese (England's oldest ally), was firstly famous for its slaves, and secondly for its role as a settlement for destitute negroes, native chiefs having ceded the peninsula to Britain in 1787 for this purpose – features of his country which Mr Sessi is too obliging to mention. Patently he is not a slave, although his great-grandfather may well have been. Mr Sessi is from the Mende tribe, in the south of the country, and this tribe, now that the Creole influence is finally broken for ever, is growing in prestige and breeding fine administrators. Perhaps he will be one of them. You can be sure that they think so at the University, and at the Embassy, which he mentions so happily, so often. No doubt the government of Sierra Leone think the money that they're paying out on Mr Sessi's education at Birmingham University, where he is probably reading sociology or social anthropology, well spent. In South Africa, Mr Sessi would be called a clever kaffir, and he would probably be doing much the same thing that he is doing in England; reading sociology or anthropology at one of the new tribal universities.

'I'm not going to talk to you for very long,' Mr Sessi explains kindly, 'and when I finish we will take a look at a film of my country, Sierra Leone, which I have had sent to the school from my embassy in London. I'd be glad if you would keep any questions that you may have until then.' He smiles charmingly. 'Your headmaster tells me that at these sessions, usually after the filmshow, you break up into groups to originate the questions you wish to put to me. I'm sure that some of them will be real stinkers! I only hope that I can oblige you with the answers when the time comes.'

His audience, though no less stony-eyed, leans forward, shoulders hunched; their sign that they are prepared to suspend judgement on Mr Sessi, in the face of such pleasantries. They have no hope that his lecture will interest them – but it just might be diverting.

Mr Sessi turns and faces the portable cinema screen that has been erected on a table at the head of the class, contemplating it with a cock of his head, this way and that, then he turns back to the waiting audience: 'Perhaps someone has a piece of chalk?' he asks diffidently, with an upward shift of the eyebrows, a flick of the head, including in his enquiry the boys and teachers who stand beside and behind them.

The Deputy Head, flustered by the request, hurries from the hall. He has no sooner disappeared through the big double doors in search of a box of chalk than a boy stands in the first row and produces from his blazer pocket a piece of chalk which he offers to Mr Sessi who beams his thanks. A murmur, of approbation I think it is, rises from his classmates who doubtless approve of this brutally swift response; natural dramatists, they appreciate any device that safeguards the smooth development of the action. Although it is impossible, it seems that Mr Sessi has mistaken the cinema screen for a blackboard.

He stands gazing at it, chalk in hand. His back is turned for a few seconds only before he faces us again. His smile continues but he makes no secret of his perplexity. His chalk hand, the right, is thrown out behind him, gesturing, as it were, towards the white screen. The murmur grows louder amongst the rows of intent boys. I won't swear to this, but it seems as if Mr Sessi is about to lose his air of good-humoured, honest confusion, and become rather quizzical. He is certainly sensitive to the unmarked silvery white screen at his back and the silent boys before him. He scrutinises the piece of chalk he holds: 'Please,' he says rather diffidently, as if he were sparing us embarrassment, 'do you write on a white board with white chalk?'

The class groans and snuffles to itself. All this, their frantic wrigglings clearly say, is too much to be borne. 'We've gorra right 'un here, all right.' It's one thing for the stupid black bugger to take a cinema screen for a blackboard, but to go so far as to offer to write on it with a piece of chalk, in good faith, is simply too good to be true. The class cast around desperately, looking for the Head, wanting to gauge his reaction to their reaction to these extraordinary goings-on. It would be unreasonable for him, their contorted expressions say, to expect from them the usual decorum he demands during these lectures. It is enough to have to stop themselves from laughing out loud.

Fighting his face muscles into a disarming, apologetic, unembarrassed smile, but reddening to the roots of his hair, the Head shuffles his slack-kneed way down the aisle and lifts up the heavy linen flap of a large Phillips map of Africa, obviously an old one, still patched in Imperial pink, which is displayed beside the cinema screen, to reveal beneath it a portable blackboard pegged on a tripod. The Deputy Head returns and hands a fistful of chalk to Mr Sessi.

'In the University,' says Mr Sessi, graciously accepting the chalks and the discovery of an orthodox blackboard with an unwavering smile and not the slightest hint of irony, 'we usually write with coloured chalks, on a white board.'

We are unprepared for the novelty of this suggestion and it gives us that faintly uncomfortable feeling we have when we catch someone out in a clumsy evasion and yet feel at the same time that to point it out to him would be more embarrassing still. So we flush, as the Head is doing, and look the other way. Yet it is a little tiresome to observe how blandly Mr Sessi ignores our scruples. I put this down to an iron nerve. God knows what the boys think of it. Probably that Mr Sessi is making a swift but silly effort to slip out of a tricky situation, choosing to make up this unlikely explanation rather than risk our scorn by admitting that he has never been face to face with a blackboard in his life. Who knows, perhaps he has never seen the inside of Birmingham University, either. Certainly he has a very thick skin if he thinks he can brazen it out like this.

At the same time I can't help wondering whether any of the boys envy Mr Sessi his black face at this moment. Surely, in one or two minds, there is the thought that the guilty blush, which to their irritation they know may spread across a face with treacherous suddenness regardless of innocence, does not show on a black face. With side-long glances I see them searching his face for the tell-tale flush. It is a waste of time, unless you know what you are looking for. Of course, black faces do blush, as any South African will tell you, and it is becoming plain to me that Mr Sessi doesn't share our embarrassment.

Some weeks later, when Mr Sessi's visit was barely remembered, I was to discover in a trade magazine an advertisement for a piece of classroom equipment described as a magnetic white marker board, the *Twinlock Saxo Whyte Bord*. Writing and drawings are accomplished with coloured marker pens. The *Wyte Bord* has an additional advantage; it can double as a cinema screen, so the advertisement claimed, and it is often used in the universities.

At the time of Mr Sessi's lecture on Sierra Leone, I will admit that I was more interested in Worcestershire than in Africa. I was living and working there, so it was the part of England most open to study. Some people associate Worcestershire with the Vale of Evesham, with apple orchards, cherries and whatnot. As a geographer I find this curious. Worcestershire, the closer one gets to Birmingham, seems to be far more factory than farm to the visitor from a less industrially developed, emptier, larger country. An area of 716 square miles with a population of some 700,000, Worcestershire melds in the north into the indistinguishability of Birmingham's environs. Villages, dispossessed by characteristic housing estates of their surrounding countryside, seem to run into one another, village into suburb, into town, into city: unsettled places floating aimlessly around and about the blast furnaces of Birmingham. This displacing instills a feeling of edginess in the inhabitants, most now drawn from the farms into the manufacturing industries, or those industries which service the manufacturing industries.

This is Worcestershire for me, perhaps for Mr Sessi too. But for both of us, this is also Africa. Simply by being here, we affect the geography of the place, we Africanise it a little. Only for a moment perhaps, but that is as long as anything lasts. This has been proved to me, as it will be to Mr Sessi, and as painfully. We are strangers to this place, quickly recognised by the natives as fearsome Captain Cooks. Since we are apparently peaceful, and come bearing gifts of novelties and wonders, they are prepared to wait before deciding what to do with us. Yet they are wary nonetheless, and hostile, in a dull, taciturn way. Men may very well be islands, as the geographer suspects, as Captain Cook learnt to his dreadful cost. And where is this more likely to prove true than on this most insular of islands?

But Mr Sessi of the Mende tribe of Sierra Leone, now of Birmingham and the University, sooner than later to be of the Civil Service, earnest and willing ambassador to the English Secondary Schools, incipient administrator, smiles on the sons of men who brush shoulders with too many of his colour in a working day to bear it without protesting: 'I'm no racialist, mind, but there's too many of them coloureds around these parts now.'

He speaks plainly and very slowly, determined to be understood. Whether he does this from long experience in a hundred school halls built to the Department of Education's uni-plan, I couldn't say. His bland, unreasonable composure offers no clue. The chances are that he has never faced an audience like this: boys of fourteen, who failed to get into Grammar school and failed thereby to qualify for any jobs but those only slightly better than black immigrants take on nowadays.

Then again, perhaps I romanticise, and all he feels up there on the rostrum is uncertainty in his new role of lecturer, and in the faces of boys who have inherited sevenfold their fathers' frustrations and fears, he sees nothing but young white students eager for a glimpse of how the other half of the world lives; and perhaps, too, his smile is really benign and falls on each equally. It is not possible for a South African to know.

'Sierra Leone is not a very big country. Now, when I say

big, I don't know what picture comes into your heads. Perhaps it will help to give you an idea of the size of Sierra Leone if I tell you that my country is not much more than half the size of England. Who knows the size of England?'

No one answers. It is unlikely that many of the class even hear the question. Resistant to language, they are still undergoing a process of adjustment to the strange presence of the speaker. It is not simply that Mr Sessi is so shiningly black and speaks a queer sort of English in a peculiar accent. No, the extraordinary thing about Mr Sessi is that he somehow manages to suggest that he is a person of some importance – to somebody. Despite his not very firm control of the language, he has an air of assurance. He doesn't speak with a Birmingham accent. It is unlikely that he comes from Bradford. He is in the country, the Head has reassured them in comforting tones before the lecture, to study. He is not an immigrant, then, and he does not speak like a coloured. They are puzzled.

Who can blame them?

He speaks English like every blackface parody from Cape Town to Baton Rouge. He is Uncle Tom, Malcolm X and Shaka, King of the Zulus, rolled up into one. And yet – he is *real*.

'Sierra Leone, you might be interested to know, has an area of 27 925 square miles. But I think that I will leave you the problem of working out from that figure how big England is by comparison,' Mr Sessi says, and his smile does not falter. 'I'm sure that you will discover that my country is a small country, relatively, but then, with only two and half million of us, we do not face the problem of over-population.'

I see the Head smiling sheepishly and he looks almost longingly at the speaker, trying to communicate his extreme sadness at the thoroughly unsuitable mode of address which Mr Sessi has chosen to adopt. To ask specific questions of these boys on any subject other than football is so novel that it might actually have succeeded in diverting the now increasingly restless class. But to expect answers from them looks like madness.

'Our climate is rather different to yours. I wonder if one of you can tell me what kind of climate you have here in Britain?'

The silence which follows this question pains me, as it will pain all geographers. More so one who has talked for weeks to these same boys in cunningly colloquial fashion, in no way resembling a geography lesson, of the vagaries of the English weather. It is specially galling to a South African to observe such ignorance in the face of black assurance, made worse because the boys are exchanging contemptuous and knowing smiles between themselves, confidently imputing the ignorance of procedure to Mr Sessi.

Yet he waits good-naturedly for an answer, and astonishingly, it comes:

'Rainy?' someone enquires tentatively.

I control an impulse to laugh. Luckily I succeed, because the boys do not laugh. In fact, from the anxious looks on their faces it appears that they are actually considering the answer, hoping that it will somehow do as a gesture of their good faith and Mr Sessi will now stop asking questions.

But Mr Sessi is unaffected. He simply replies, 'No, no — temperate, I would say.'

Merely by extracting an answer, Mr Sessi has scored, and it rankles. To prolong my chagrin, I go over in my mind all that I know of Sierra Leone, the last of the English monarchical possessions in Africa. It is no longer a country which holds significance for Britain and thus for the world at large. The industrious slavers who worked their monopolies so successfully are dead, gone and forgotten. When slaving was found to be no longer viable as an industry, those patriarchs, that is to say, their imperial bookkeepers, allowed the trade to be written off and did not object when the imperial abolitionists turned it to their credit. Sierra Leone, with its apt capital of Freetown, became the settling place of freed slaves from America, Europe and the surrounding colonies in Africa. They put their freedom to the test by cohabiting with the white settlers of Sierra Leone. The Creoles, born of this union, learnt the craft of government from their British masters. When the British began to leave, it was the Creoles who took over the job of administering the indigenous tribes, from Freetown with its excellent harbour, once a Second-Class Imperial Coaling Station. Now the Creoles are in decline. It is Mr Sessi of the Mende tribe who is being groomed for the business of administration. For the tribes of Sierra Leone are a little fractious, and need proper government.

'You must understand that I come from what is known as a developing country, in the Third World. Please realise that as you in Britain have had your industrial revolution, we are just beginning now to have ours. We are learning to stand on our own two feet. And if Sierra Leone is to progress and to take her rightful place among the free nations, people in faraway countries must get out of their minds the notion that we are a small uninteresting country offering no more than a good harbour and exportable crops of kernels, nuts and palm oil.'

Mr Sessi's longest speech: I find myself nodding in agreement or sympathy, I'm not sure which. It is plain that Mr Sessi is sentimentally attached to his former colonial masters. He pays them the compliment of studying at one of their newer universities, aping their manners and dress, and continually comparing with just the right amount of patriotic pride and fervour his homeland with the Old Country. By the standards of diplomacy, he is inarticulate, but then he is young, and will soon improve out of all recognition. This lecture to this speechless class in a secondary modern school in semi-rural Worcestershire is good practice for a man who will one day have charge of an area the size of this county and who will have to deal with tribes no less sullen, inarticulate and suspicious than the young men he now faces.

Does it occur to him, I ask myself, that the British have no one left to administer but themselves, nowhere left to direct their energies? Mr Sessi from post-Imperial black Africa stands lecturing this bored, incomprehending audience of resentful, truculent and occasionally dangerous young men who chafe at school discipline – so like colonial paternalism – on the complexities of familial and tribal structures, and the difficulties of administering mutually antagonistic tribes in a huge country.

'In Sierra Leone we have only two seasons in the year. Can one of you tell me how many seasons you have here in Britain? You have four, right? Who knows what they are called? No one? Well, for a start there is spring – now, which are the others? Summer, that's right, well done, and . . . ? Come on, now. What about autumn? Right! And the last one . . . ?'

Obviously the spell which Mr Sessi's performance before the cinema screen cast upon the audience has worn off. No one answers him. But he is undeterred.

'You see, where you in Britain have four seasons a year, we in Sierra Leone have only two – the rainy season and the dry season. Now, is there anyone here who knew that? Hands up!' He delivers the injunction like an actor in a gangster film.

Obviously the Head finds the breathy silence that follows this remark more than he can bear. He stands. 'It's very unlikely that we could accustom ourselves to the extreme climate which you experience in Sierra Leone. Luckily your people are bred to withstand it.'

I have the feeling that he means this as a compliment, and a salutary reflection for the boys to ponder on in case they feel too cocky about their own toughness. He considers strength of character to be the best of virtues.

Mr Sessi says nothing, but waits politely for the Head to finish talking. The Head continues: 'We don't always realise, enjoying as we do a temperate climate, what rigours of weather must be faced by people living in the wilder parts of the globe. How harsh the conditions must be for a white man unused to great heat, dust or tropical rainstorms. The very worst that we in Britain have to worry about is a cold winter.'

He has given up the meagre pretence of including Mr Sessi in his remarks and is now talking directly to the boys. He is talking with that tone of voice, cock of his head, hunch of his shoulders, very pose of a none too bright but nonetheless articulate, properly English, uncle, which he affects on occasions when his students are baffled by something outside their range of experience. He manages to soothe without subjecting them to the stress of having to digest new information, while at the same time appearing to be teaching them something. To those who know him, his demeanour also suggests a rebuke to the speaker for his handling of the lecture and manages to imply that by smoothing over the unsightly gulf yawning between Mr Sessi and his audience he has earned our gratitude. The effect of his intervention is to reassure the boys that all is well, despite this black man's strange behaviour; that England, in the guise of this northern corner of Worcestershire near Birmingham, still stands. Mr Sessi has only made a temporary incursion upon this stable place. Soon he will be gone and by tomorrow or the next day, the Head's tone promises them, they will have forgotten all about him. But in the meantime, it is surely not too much to ask that they put up with his strange manners. He will be quick to step in and iron out any misunderstandings, they can feel sure of that. Besides, his look says, we must know, just as he does, that the black man is not really odd, but only appears so to us.

The Head's demeanour leaves none of this unsaid. The class is calm again, for a while. While he speaks, we all, boys and teachers, gaze at the floor, sneaking glances at him. When he finishes, we can look Mr Sessi in the eye again. No one in the hall has listened to what he has said, except perhaps Mr Sessi, but the fact that he has spoken brings comfort.

I am uneasily aware how my identity as a white South African, were it known to Mr Sessi, will alter his conception of his audience. As it is, I felt uneasy when the Head talked of the difficulties white settlers have with lousy weather. Remarks like this often have the boys in assembly turning round to gawp at me. They do so whenever anything is mentioned which is associated in their minds with the other side of the world, however oblique the reference, whether to missionaries, David Livingstone, the Dark Continent, Zulu Chiefs or Witch Doctors. When their attention is too pointedly drawn to their own country, it has much the same effect. Goggling heads on craning necks stare at me as if my foreignness reassures them that universes other than their own really do exist, for I stand as living proof of them. Perhaps they are grateful for this because it means that they do not have to take on trust everything they see on television.

Mr Sessi shows no resentment at the Head's interruption. He seems anxious to get on with his lecture. But I notice that he has stopped smiling. I am beginning to feel something for Mr Sessi. His English is no more than makeshift, his assurance is irritating, his knowledge of the geography of his own country is limited. But in this depressing school hall, he is someone with whom I feel a kinship. I would like to reach out and touch him. However, he might not like that. Certainly such behaviour would be novel and unwelcome. I am the geography master. I might seem eccentric because I am from Africa and the boys confuse my foreignness with eccentricity, and in their unplumbable ignorance are moved to play superstitious, rather giggly aborigines to my Captain Cook. My trinkets are welcome diversions in the monotony of their prison island. But if I dared to express my sense of closeness with Mr Sessi, I'd immediately be damned as a lunatic. I am expected to show myself in every important respect to be British. So too, of course, is Mr Sessi.

At times like this I am always grateful for my training which has taught me to stick to the facts. I am most at home with geographical facts. The Republic of South Africa lies at the southern tip of the African continent. It was once a refreshment station of the Dutch East India Company; later the gold mine of the British Empire. In an area some five times that of Great Britain there are 21,448,169 people of varying colours of skin – not only black and white, but the varying intermediate colours of Bushmen, Hottentots, Chinese, Japanese, Malays and Englishmen.

These are the facts. I verify them in my books. I am sure of them. I have many more at my fingertips.

Mr Sessi is still talking, but more incoherently now. If only his sense of geography were better and he knew where he was. He is explaining the role of the chief in the tribes of Sierra Leone, quite oblivious to the fact that he has lost his audience. He talks to us as equals; working on the assumption, no doubt encouraged at his university, and his embassy for that matter, that in academic matters at least skin colour plays no part. It's not going to help him with these boys. They are pragmatists. They admit only the evidence of their senses. They accept only those illusions which entertain them.

But the good-humoured interrogation does not stop, or even wind down. Mr Sessi is deaf to the widespread, almost frantic fidgeting, of the boys and the soft shrieks of the rubber-tipped chair legs on the floorboards. But we hear it.

The Head intervenes again. He senses that the boys are on the point of mutiny. He is on his feet and talking before anyone is aware of it. We turn interestedly to see him newly risen from his chair, right foot flung forward giving the impression of leaning into a stride while standing still, his right hand raised with two fingers erect in a gesture recalling papal benediction, or absolution, his face pink and earnest beneath its cap of silver-grey hair.

'I think perhaps we could have the film now,' he is saying, 'and after that we will divide the class up into their groups for a question-and-answer session.'

Mr Sessi stops in mid-sentence as the Head's voice reaches him. 'Oh, yes . . .' he says, 'but of course, the film, of course.' He casts around desperately behind him, fluttering his eyelashes at the blackboard, then at the cinema screen.

'Would you care to sit here, perhaps?' The Head indicates a seat beside him. Mr Sessi makes his way down the aisle between the rows of boys, smiling and nodding from side to side. The Head signals to the boy operating the projector, and gives me a meaningful glance. I walk to the back of the hall and switch off the lights. A greenish twilight settles on the hall. Things darken to a blur.

The film is barely on the screen before we realise that it is not what we had hoped. However hard we may have longed for the kindness of darkness to allow us to relax into the pleasant distractions of faraway Sierra Leone, after the assaults of the indefatigable Mr Sessi, there is to be no rest for us in the flickering images on the screen. This is not what we expected: the public relations creation of colourful native life, the import of industrial plant and motor cars, the export of palm oil, nuts and kernels for which the country is famed, together with unusual views of derricks and cranes in Freetown harbour, and ships with recognisable Union Jacks on their funnels being loaded with the country's fruits by singing stevedores, and everywhere the smiling black faces of happy Sierra Leonians. Instead I am staring at the broad back of a white man sitting across a table from an earnest, bespectacled black man. Both are talking at once. It seems that we are being exposed to another interrogation. The sound track is muddy and very noisy. Yet it approximates to the sound of human voices in conversation, and instinctively I try to make out what is being said. The black man is doing most of the talking. His lips move rapidly, he shifts in his chair, giving the other's questions serious consideration before replying lengthily. The film is in black and white and the print is grainy. After five long minutes of this I am suddenly certain that the scene will not alter while the projector continues to run. The boys slump miserably in the darkness. Rubber chair legs begin their cries again. Blurred white faces turn to the back of the hall where the Head and Mr Sessi sit side by side in the darkness. I can see him conferring with Mr Sessi who is nodding a great deal. The Head whispers to the projectionist and the conversationalists fade from the screen. I walk to the back of the hall and switch on the light. Everyone blinks furiously, rubbing their eyes, hiding their embarrassment so painfully renewed. The Head is on his feet again, his head bobbing about the way a hen's does, vigilant for any sign of trouble. Mr Sessi remains seated. His head hangs low. The Head calls for silence.

'We're going to stop the film there. Hmm, yes, we have to end it, I'm afraid. Mr Sessi tells me that there appears to have been a misunderstanding. Got the film at the last moment, you see, and didn't have time to check it. Took it for granted, hmm, that the people at his embassy in London knew what they were doing. As you'll have noticed, seems somebody has slipped up. This was, hmm, a political film, dealing with the trade union movement in Sierra Leone and, er, its relationship with the International Labour Organisation. Not really your cup of tea, ha, as Mr Sessi himself was quick to point out. I'm sorry, of course, you'll have no glimpse of Sierra Leone after the valuable insights of Mr Sessi's lecture. But these things happen.'

Mr Sessi rises slowly to his feet. Giving the Head a little bow he walks up to the head of the class and takes up a position in front of the cinema screen, with his hands behind his back. Clearly he is unhappy. He has a hang-dog look to him now. He clears his throat. He appears to be having trouble with his eyes, passing his hand across them – when he speaks, his voice is soft: 'In view of what has happened, for which I cannot apologise too much, I think you can dispense with your usual discussion groups. In the time remaining, I will simply invite questions from the floor.' There is no response. For a moment he stands silently, with his head drooping almost to his breast; then he straightens and it looks as if he has regained some of his old cheerfulness. At any rate, he faces all of us unflinchingly.

'All right,' he says, 'fire away.'

Whatever Happened to Vilakazi?

All I know for sure is that he went missing sometime between the Saturday evening before Quinquagesima Sunday (which in that year, so clearly do I remember, fell on the 3rd of March) and the following Wednesday, Ash Wednesday. In that dark, devouring time as the Church bares itself and makes ready for the chastisement of the Lenten days ahead my thoughts were turning, even more swiftly than usual, to the prospect of sudden death, about which there was a lot of seasonal talk in catechism lessons, and you were either like Billy Hendriks who, though he was also an altar server, called the whole thing a lot of bally tripe, or you were like Bastable who had been knocked down and killed earlier that year, shortly after he'd been to confession, and was held up as an example of a very lucky boy, or you were like me, secretly admiring Hendriks' nerve while expecting Bastable's fate, without his luck. As the reminders of mortality piled up that week, my fears grew, fatally drawing me into the church for a devotional visit on the Saturday evening after a game of badminton with Hendriks in the parish hall which he'd won despite the fact that he was so bad he held his racket in both hands and had only one stroke, a pushing shot beginning at his nose and ending at his knees.

It was in the darkened church through clasped fingers that I saw the strange figure at the altar rails. The sight dismayed and frightened me, it made me feel guilty and yet, helpless, so much so that when there was no sign of the boy on the Sunday morning around the parish gardens or the vestry door, I was actually rather relieved. But when there was still no sign of him by Wednesday I knew I had to do something, and besides too many of the other servers had noticed his disappearance to ignore it.

Even then I delayed until school was out; I might have gone after mass that morning. On Ash Wednesday it was customary for the entire school to make its way to the parish church where Father Besserman assisted by two priests carrying large white porcelain urns moved up and down the altar rails where nearly five hundred boys knelt piously with their fists kneading their closed eyes, breathing the smell of starch in the white altar cloth covering the rails, newly washed by Brother Musel, and felt the priest lightly sign with his thumb the fatal mark on their foreheads and heard the murmured reminder that man was dust and unto dust he would return. I felt Father Besserman's crisp touch, like footsteps on cinders magnified in my ears and heard his whispered Latin prophecy of my mortality, saw behind my eyelids the black draped bier in the aisle and the six tall candles of my own mass for the dead, now surely very near, and made my way back to my pew wrinkling my forehead gently in a reverent effort to feel the cross of ash Father Besserman had printed there.

I might have gone to see him after mass about the missing boy, but still I delayed. Maybe he'd turn up, I told myself, without much hope in my heart. For the rest of that day one tended to avert one's eyes from one's friends; it was hard to see them as condemned men. There was an unwritten law forbidding you to rub out your cross, you had to wait for the wind and your hair and the natural erasure of daily wear. Usually by early afternoon it was safe to begin looking your friends in the face again as by then usually only the ashy ghosts of crosses remained, dark smudges, wispy flakes caught in the eyebrows, and you breathed more easily, seeing your friends no longer as creatures marked for death but merely as boys with dirty foreheads.

After school I went to see Father Besserman because Hendriks and the others said that if I didn't they would and so I had no option, feeling dreadfully obliged to do so anyway since I knew more than any of them and the weight of my knowledge depressed and wearied me.

Father Besserman was pitiless in his kindly understanding: 'He was a stray and you can't make pets of such creatures. He has gone as he arrived – without our consent.'

'But he's a boy, Father. Something may have happened.'

He put his arm around my shoulders. 'To you he's a boy. To me he's a boy, maybe, but in fact he's really a man. Made strong by the street. Maybe he went back to his friends. His pack.'

He knew what I was thinking when he used that word because he said, 'If you like ask Brother Musel. He's good at keeping an eye on boys, not so?'

'Brother Musel didn't like him. Brother Musel threw stones at him.'

Father Besserman frowned but did not contradict me. 'All the more reason why maybe he is the last to see him, *ja*?'

Brother Musel looked after the altar boys and he looked after the rich garments in the vestry, the gorgeous copes picked out in their holy geometry of gold and silver thread; he folded and handled and watched over, too, the deep brown drawers and cupboards housing maniples and chasubles, the candlesticks, the supplies of hosts and the sacramental wine, the dully gleaming chalices; and he took in all the laundry that needed doing and washed and dried it down in his boiler room where he stoked the great furnace that fed the boiler. Square-headed, grizzled around the jaws, he was launderer, janitor, sacristan, master of the altar boys and general dogsbody to the superior fathers of the order. His face was deeply lined, remote and deceptively dreamy for he was not a gentle man. The broad capable hands, the great muscles got by shovelling coal and his capacity for continuous hard work were always noticeable. He had a habit of humming to himself. As you pulled your black cassock and your white surplice on one side of the wooden panelling you could hear Brother Musel at work on the other, folding, hanging and tidying, humming above the clash of the big wooden hangers and the somehow deeply reassuring 'clock-clock' of the birettas as Brother Musel slid each winged black hat home into the deep shelf in the cupboard where the copes were hung.

The priests of our parish were a German order and had settled in the area some twenty years before and so escaped the war, which was just as well, Billy Hendriks liked to say, because some of them would have made first-grade SS material. What I think he meant by that was that the German priests were so superior, clearly and effortlessly superior, to the local Europeans, and the Africans were simply beneath their notice; they exuded a peculiar kind of confidence which none of us could hope to match; though everyone we knew had been bred also to feel superior, in our case I think it was more a question of struggling always not to feel inferior. We had no confidence, our confidence had been undermined early by the poison of racialism which we took in with our mother's milk and so, whereas a salutary sense of themselves came naturally to the German priests, it was something we had to fight for; there was for us nothing like a natural hierarchy, to us social structure was war. I remember Audrey Hiemstra trying to explain to Father Besserman why she objected to a suggestion by some deranged liberal member of the congregation that the brass plaques on the four final pews in the church marked 'Reserved', so designating them for the use of Africans only, should be removed and Africans be allowed to sit where they liked. Mrs Hiemstra objected to this idea because, frankly, she told Father Besserman she was not prepared to sit beside black people or to allow her daughter to do so and as for her husband, well, she shuddered to think how he would react if he found himself in coloured company, since, she reminded him, her husband was, frankly, a mine manager and quite capable of taking offence at the slightest look, gesture or, here she paused delicately, odor, and thrashing the offending African right there and then, place of worship or not, sorry as she was, frankly, to have to admit it. She added that, of course, she didn't expect Father Besserman to understand or share or approve of her attitude, and again, frankly, she didn't care whether he did or not, but he had to understand how 'her' people felt about these things. She was white, she was very sorry about that, but there it was and she didn't believe everyone was created equal or wanted to be, or would ever be, nor did any of her family or friends. In an effort to reassure her, Father Besserman told her that he felt he understood exactly what she meant, even though, as he would be the first to admit, he hadn't been born in Africa, but in fact he confessed very cordially to feeling exactly the same about the Poles . . . What this admission achieved was to underline Father Besserman's incapacity for understanding things the way we did – all the same she was grateful to him for making the effort. 'Father Besserman doesn't like the Poles, you know,' she would tell people loudly after Sunday morning mass and they would nod cheerfully without any idea of what she meant, gathering from her tone that the man was doing his best.

Father Besserman, the rector, had a shining pink dome of a head on a short pink neck, stout as a surgical collar; a fair, firm, almost genial man; certainly in comparison with Brother Musel he was a radiant light and it was his benign neglect which allowed Vilakazi to stay on, to gradually attach himself to the church when the general consensus among the rest of the priests would have been to boot him back across the hedge through which he had slipped into the gutter from where he had come when Billy and I found him on our way to serve early morning mass. He was curled up under a loquat tree fast asleep. I don't think we'd ever seen a child asleep in the open air on a brisk Highveld morning. All he had on was a pair of shorts, a man's white shirt too large for him and an old sports coat. I remember we stared at his bare feet, at hard-skinned, scaley soles with dust in the cracks and were struck by the fact that he was about the same age as we were. We couldn't get over that. We knew what he was, of course, he was a *piccanin*, a scamp from the streets, a young beggar, the sort of fellow who touched you for pennies in town, who joined with others into tattered orchestras for Christmas, playing their penny whistles and their biscuit tin drums and their primitive basses made from tea chest, broomstick handles and a string to strum, when, since they were an ingredient in the annual seasonal spirit, they were regarded as picturesque, though for the rest of the time they were acknowledged to be an unsightly and irritating nuisance.

On that first morning when we came out of mass he was cleaning our bikes with the end of his shirt sleeve; when he saw us he stood back with a smile and a flourish and stuck out his hand. Billy Hendriks gave him a cigarette and the boy tucked it behind his ear.

'What's your name?'

The boy tapped his chest. 'Vilakazi'.

Brother Musel appeared on the sacristy steps and bawled at us to report to him on the double and to bring black mischief along. He marched us off holding the frightened boy by his thin neck and paraded us before a bemused Father Besserman who, probably because he wasn't at all sure what was expected of him and perhaps as an evidence of good faith pointed at the cigarette behind his ear and invited him to smoke, ordering Brother Musel to give the boy a light, which the sacristan grudgingly did from the giant box he carried in his pocket for lighting the boiler furnace. We watched Vilakazi inhaling gratefully, openly smoking in front of adults in a way we would never dare to have done and envying him a certain freedom though envy could not go very far, not with us standing in our coats and our gloves and Vilakazi in his torn pants and bare feet, nodding every so often and politely collecting the ash in his palm, appearing to listen intently while Father Besserman told him that he might not remain on church property and must leave immediately. The boy smiled and nodded heartily though I think all of us realised he didn't understand what he heard and then we all went out of the church gates and Brother Musel sternly pointed Vilakazi into the distance. We watched him walking away with his head slightly bowed. Brother Musel smacked his hands together with an air of satisfaction which seemed excessive.

That night he was back; Brother Musel had spotted him when he rose before dawn to light the boiler and charged after him with his shovel. Vilakazi had bolted and he hadn't been able to catch him. 'But I got close enough to hit the little devil with a good stone – here on the back.' He jabbed a thumb between his shoulder blades. There was something deeply shaming in the picture of big Brother Musel pursuing the boy through the garden and throwing stones at him that made us flinch and shiver and so when we came out of mass and found Vilakazi waiting for us, smiling as broadly as ever and seemingly none the worse for it, all of us were hugely relieved and I think it was then in effect that we decided, though we said nothing about it, to defend him as far as that was possible, in a sense to adopt him.

Gradually it became known to all the priests and to all the congregation that Vilakazi inhabited the garden and this unspoken fact was accepted by everyone except Brother Musel. He showed his dissatisfaction in various ways. He became even more scrupulous about the cleanliness of our cassocks and surplices, about the security of the wine and the wafers, about the locks on the great oak doors of the vestment cupboard and he would stride into the vestry in the early morning smelling of cinders from the furnace and soap from the laundry, his face flushed with the flames and steam of the place and reach into the cupboards twitching our surplices on their wire hangers, testing for dirt and humming deeply up and down a scale as if trying to remember an old tune. He had the sense to realise that the rest of the community were on Vilakazi's side, feeling that if the boy had the strength to stick it out he should be allowed somehow to stay on. He didn't rage against him but he never let the matter rest.

'They travel in groups, these boys. Like stray dogs, in packs. You let one in and soon you'll have the whole pack sleeping in the garden. It was like that in the old days on my father's estate.'

'Our Father's house has many mansions, Brother Musel,' said Father Besserman with an inclination of his head towards us, reminding his sacristan that the altar boys present expected conversation among priests to have a religious tone to it.

'We have only one garden,' Brother Musel pointed out reasonably. 'In my father's place we found one day a single badger. What harm could a single badger do? That's what we asked. Soon the garden was full of badgers.'

'A single boy is scarcely a garden full of badgers,' Father Besserman said, carefully amiable.

'In the end we had to gas them, those badgers. My father, he kept many cows. The badgers were infecting the cows. They gave them tuberculosis.'

Vilakazi must have known how delicate his position was and he kept low though he was always there when we arrived to serve mass, or for Wednesday novena or the Sunday benediction, smiling as if we were old friends with never a care in the world, but too wise not to understand his difficult position. He wasn't content simply to stay in the garden, he worked at establishing himself there, he tried to turn himself into the gardener and he'd go around sweeping up the leaves and pulling weeds and generally keeping everything tidy though he had no tools. He pulled the weeds by hand and I'd seen him sweeping, using a handful of branches as a broom, or on the pathway even using his bare feet. We approved of this; if he was going to stay then he would have to look as if he belonged, for belonging, we knew, was very much a question of appearances. There was in the corner of the garden, down by the hedge and beneath the great fir trees, a pump-house controlling the water supply, it was in this that Vilakazi took up residence. The place was damp and smelt of oil and trembled with the thudding engine, but he appropriated it and no one objected. His bed consisted of an old tennis net, doubled and redoubled on the floor: on the wall were colour photographs torn from old magazines showing obscure South American rugby teams, all red shirts and big grins and folded arms, an old pair of bicycle handlebars he'd found somewhere and hung like chromium antlers on the wall, and a picture of a priest in his glory, dazzling in a crimson cope shot with silver thread, scalloped, embellished and glowing; this picture of the priest gave us an insight into what fascinated him about us because it was clear that even in our plain black and white cassocks and surplices we beguiled him and he loved nothing more than to take the edging of lace on the cuff between his finger and rub it gently against his cheek talking in his language which we didn't understand.

I'd like to say that we got to know him well and, at a level below conversation, perhaps we did but his English never got any better and he never put on weight, darting through the bushes like the stray Musel said he was, scraggy, easily scared, endlessly cheerful, always begging for a cigarette and never looking much other than the little guy Hendriks and I had found asleep under the loquat tree. We brought him clothes, blankets and food, sometimes money and often cigarettes. I think we saw these gifts as our only weapons, outward signs and even warnings to Musel that we watched over Vilakazi.

On the Saturday evening before Quinquagesima Sunday I paid a visit to the church after playing a game of badminton with Hendriks in the parish hall next door and which I'd lost unnecessarily. My nerves were especially ragged. The nights that last week had been bad for this was the time I was going to sleep convinced that each night was my last, that I'd choke, or my heart would stop, or a vein would burst inside my head. I was quite convinced, or at least one part of me was convinced, and another part of me prayed wildly that the fate might be lifted from me, while yet a third part of me stood somewhat aside and watched sceptically to see what was going to happen, judging that while I was able to go on talking there must still be life in me and if I kept on talking long enough death might be slipped. I was praying almost constantly at the time, making visits to the church on every possible occasion and on the Saturday evening I threw myself down on my knees in the porch and prayed. The church was in darkness but the red light burning continuously before the tabernacle threw a glow across the altar steps and rail and a little moonlight pushed through the stone windows of the Lady Chapel, showing the portrait of the Byzantine virgin in her swirling circles of gold and blue, clutching her wide-eyed child.

I was about to leave when I saw him. He came out of the door leading from the vestry. At first I thought I was having a dream or a vision. He wore a cope. It seemed from where I was green, dark green with gold markings, and he walked very slowly and very quietly. Of course he had no shoes on, I remembered, and this slowness and silence gave him a strange and frightening dignity even though the cope was far too big and swept behind him, hissing across the parquet flooring as he moved up to the altar rails where he knelt and bowed his head; he knelt there a minute or two perhaps and then stood and opened the little wooden gate and moved up towards the altar itself. He stood in front of the tabernacle. I am sure his face was shining, except, of course, I never saw his face. Never again. I couldn't watch any more and getting very quietly to my feet I slipped from the church.

When Father Besserman insisted Vilakazi had gone back to his own kind, I would have dearly like to believe him. Instead I asked where I could find Brother Musel. Father Besserman, relieved of the responsibility, kept his arm around my shoulders and walked me into the vestry. We found it empty, cupboard doors ajar, smelling of beeswax, floor polish, disinfectant. Father Besserman chuckled. 'He's having a spring-cleaning. That's it. He is a shining man, Brother Musel. Scrupulous. You know what scrupulous means?'

'It's not spring, Father, it's nearly autumn.'

But there was no way past his implacable amiability. 'Yes. In Africa. But Brother Musel is a European at heart and in Europe now it's nearly spring. Go look for him in the boiler room. Maybe he never saw your friend, but it won't hurt to ask.'

The boiler room in the basement was large and brick-lined. Brother Musel was ironing a cassock on a big trestle table, the cloth flowing under the iron. The place was heavy with steam and the smell of soap and cinders. The clean surplices strung on a washing line across the room, stretched by their arms on the pegs, white, flaccid and somehow helpless, billowing gently in the currents of hot air from the furnace. The boiler hissed and ticked. Brother Musel went on ironing, his cassock sleeves rolled up above the elbow and the bunching muscles round as eggs gliding beneath the skin of his forearms. The furnace behind him kept up a slow steady roar and I could see through the observation window the coals banked up and gleaming fiercely, rich and ruddy like pirates' gold in picture books.

'Here is a cassock.' He handed me the cassock he'd been ironing, damply warm. 'Take a surplice from the line. Any one. All are clean. What I could not wash has gone to the dry-cleaning. Everything is clean here now.' He set the iron on its stand where it stood ticking, a smaller quicker sound than that the boiler gave off. Again that hum of his, a deep, tuneless, searching, as if he probed his own hidden depths. Then I noticed the picture. It was the photograph of a priest torn from a magazine. It lay beside the iron on the table.

'The boy is missing.'

'What boy is that?'

I grew restless, his studied indifference made me want to provoke him.

'I saw him on Saturday night.'

He shrugged, the humming deepened.

'It was in church, at the altar.'

'That cannot be. You are mistaken.'

'He was wearing a set of vestments and I think he carried a chalice.'

The terrible humming stopped. 'Are you mad? A native boy at the altar? I was in church on Saturday night. I was keeping a vigil before the tabernacle. I saw nobody. You're making a joke with me, a bad, impious joke.'

'Where is Vilakazi, Brother Musel?'

'Why do you ask me?'

I pointed to the picture. 'That belonged to him.'

He picked up the picture. 'This I find in the pump-house. A pin had been driven through it. I suspect stray natives who plague the garden by night; stupid, ignorant people making witchcraft, voodoo. You know voodoo?'

'The boy lived in the pump-house.'

The large, calm eyes regarded me. 'What boy?'

'The boy who owned the picture.'

He stared at me long and hard and then with a sudden movement he picked up the picture and deliberately crushed it. Screwing it up in his hand, holding his big, white-knuckled fist in the air between us and as if this was a ceremony, he crossed to the furnace, opened the door and threw the ball of paper inside where it flared on the golden coals, unclenched, and slowly died. Closing the door he turned his unsmiling face to me. 'What picture?'

I took my cassock and surplice smelling hot and clean, pressed it to my chest and went back to the sacristy. In the mirror I examined my face for signs of the knowledge I knew I carried within me. My face, as I'd half hoped, showed nothing of what it knew, though I could not make it meet my eyes. For an instant I almost persuaded myself that I owed it to that smooth, untroubled young face not to betray the innocence I saw there. It does not know, I said to myself, bending forward, and so you cannot know . . . then my nose touched the mirror and squinting upwards I saw, faintly darkening my forehead, the last few minute flakes of what had been my cross of ash.